# And Maggie
# Makes Three

# And Maggie Makes Three

JOAN LOWERY NIXON

Harcourt Brace Jovanovich, Publishers

*San Diego    New York    London*

Requests for permission to make copies
of any part of the work should be mailed to:
Permissions, Harcourt Brace Jovanovich, Publishers,
Orlando, Florida 32887

Printed in the United States of America

LIBRARY OF CONGRESS CATALOGING-IN-PUBLICATION DATA

Nixon, Joan Lowery.
And Maggie makes three.

Summary: Twelve-year-old Maggie, living with her
grandmother in Houston, joins the drama club at school,
wins a part in a play, begins to make friends,
and learns to deal with feelings of loneliness,
selfishness, being in love, and having an
unusual family life and background.
[1. Grandmothers—Fiction.
2. Fathers and daughters—Fiction.
3. Schools—Fiction. 4. Plays—Fiction.
5. Friendship—Fiction] I. Title.
PZ7.N65An 1986 [Fic] 85-16389

ISBN 0-15-250355-2

Designed by Michael Farmer

First edition

A B C D E

FOR VERONICA MARY
WITH MY LOVE

# And Maggie
# Makes Three

# 1

Maggie Ledoux stood on the red-brick sidewalk in front of
Greely Middle School and watched the blinking red taillights
of Grandma's blue sedan as it stopped at the corner, turned,
and disappeared in Westheimer Boulevard traffic.

The all-alone feeling was like a frozen Popsicle stuck
in the middle of her stomach, and she pressed her hand there,
wishing the feeling would go away.

Eventually, it would. Maggie knew that from experience.
At each new school it was always the same. New teachers;
girls with unfriendly, staring faces; strange rules to get used
to—and a movie-director father living hundreds of miles away.
At least here in Houston she had a home with Grandma.

Grandma. Maggie took a deep breath.

"Since I'm just going to live with you a year, I can study
at home," Maggie had told her grandmother. "Then I won't
have to go to school at all."

"There are laws," Grandma had answered. "Besides, in
school you'll find lots of nice girls your age. You'll want to
meet them and make friends."

Maggie had scowled. "Remember? I told you I don't make friends."

"Why not? You're the kind of person *I'd* like to have for a friend."

"Just you, Grandma. Nobody else. Anyhow, I never stay in a school very long, so why bother."

Grandma had run her fingers through her short red-brown hair as she studied Maggie. Then she said, "Sometimes when people feel shy about trying to make friends, they try to cover up their shyness by pretending they really don't care."

"I don't want to talk about it!" Maggie had answered.

So Grandma had said, "All right. Your father's secretary mailed all the papers you'll need to enroll in Greely, so we'll leave a little early on Wednesday and visit the seventh-grade counselor's office before I go to my school for its orientation day."

Maggie wished she was still in fifth grade so that she could go to the elementary school where Grandma was a librarian. She felt so cross and unhappy and mixed-up that she complained, "I'm twelve years old, Grandma. Almost thirteen. I can enroll in school by myself!"

So, because of her big mouth, here she was all alone in front of Greely Middle School, feeling so scared that she wanted to turn around and run.

She wished she had worn her jeans. Lots of the kids were wearing jeans. Grandma had told her that jeans would be fine. But she had insisted on wearing her new, striped cotton dress because in it she looked as though she had lost even more than the eight pounds she had already lost while she'd been here in Houston. Now the dress felt stiff and uncomfortable.

Two girls passed her so closely on the sidewalk that she had to move back quickly, stumbling a little as she stepped onto the grass. For a moment they looked at her, then went back to their conversation. Feeling clumsy and awkward, Maggie turned to follow them toward the central door of the main building.

A group of laughing, yelling boys, poking and socking each other as they ran, suddenly surrounded Maggie. She clutched her notebook and handbag to her chest and squeezed her eyes shut in terror. When nothing happened, she opened her eyes to discover that the boys had shoved their way to the steps leading to the main door and were disappearing inside the school building.

Boys! She shuddered. She had always boarded at all-girl schools. She had never gone to a public school, never been in a school with boys. It was bad enough to have to exist every day with girls she didn't like and who wouldn't like her. It would be even worse with boys.

Others were arriving. She had to get this over with sooner or later. Maggie stood up a little straighter and entered Greely Middle School, following the arrows that pointed up the stairs to the second floor office of the counselor for the seventh grade.

The chairs in the small room were filled, mostly with an assortment of what looked like mothers, while their kids stood between the chairs, leaning against the walls and trying to look inconspicuous.

Slumped in the nearest chair was a pimply-faced boy with long legs, who shot them out as Maggie came close. But Maggie knew that trick. She had once been in trouble for trying it herself, back in sixth grade in Miss Haversham's School for Girls. So she calmly stepped over his legs, went to the desk, took a folder of papers from her notebook, and held it out.

A woman with straggly brown hair, who looked as though

she'd rather be anywhere else at the moment, tried to smile at Maggie and said, "School records? Last report card? Medical record? Had all your shots?"

"All except rabies and distemper," Maggie said.

The woman's smile flickered, as though she weren't sure if Maggie were joking, and the boy in the chair snorted.

"It looks okay, Margaret," the woman said. She quickly thumbed through the papers in Maggie's folder. "Sit down somewhere, and we'll get to you in a moment."

Maggie walked to the only blank wall space left and leaned against it. A girl, whose eyes were as brightly blue as the shirt she was wearing, turned to Maggie. "You new here, too?" She kept twisting a strand of her long brown hair around one finger.

Maggie nodded.

"We came down from Jersey," the girl said. "More jobs here than up east. Is that why you're here?"

"No," Maggie said.

The girl, still twisting her hair, just looked at her, as though waiting for an answer. Maggie wished she could tell her why she was living for a year with her grandmother, and why her father had sent her here, having recently married a twenty-year-old starlet who didn't want the responsibility of a twelve-year-old girl. She couldn't. Nobody would understand how she felt about Kiki and her father. She was lonely in this strange school, but it wasn't for her father, who was still in Italy because of delays in filming the movie he was directing. She was lonely for the grandmother she had learned to love.

The mother and son across the room were called to the desk, and the girl with the blue eyes took the empty chair. She didn't look in Maggie's direction again. Maggie tried to think of something to say to start a conversation again, but it didn't seem to be worthwhile. The girl wouldn't want to be friends anyway.

Maggie watched the room begin to empty as the woman at the desk checked records and gave out class schedules and directions for finding homerooms. Finally it was her turn.

"Everything's in order," the woman said, and she scribbled furiously on a class schedule form. A bell jangled loudly in the hall. She waited for the noise to end, then handed the paper to Maggie. "Sixth grade orientation must be over," she said. "You can go right to your homeroom. That's the first room number on your list. Mrs. Hardison's your homeroom teacher. I've got your other classes listed in order and time. You can get your locker key in homeroom. Any questions?"

"Yes," Maggie said. "What am I doing here?"

"I ask myself that every day," the woman said. She picked up a sheet of paper and peered around Maggie. "Richard Enderly?" she called.

Maggie squeezed past the heavy-set woman who piloted a short, chubby boy to the desk. She opened the door to the hall and joined a mass of pushing, hurrying, chattering, laughing people. The hall smelled of fresh paint, old gym clothes, stale bubblegum, and now and then a whiff of sticky cologne.

"Yuck!" Maggie said, and, "Ouch!" as someone tromped on her foot. Holding her sheet of paper tightly and using her elbows to keep from getting stomped on again, she managed to find her homeroom. She hurried inside the door and slipped into a seat at the far back corner.

A tall woman, young enough to wear her hair in a tightly clipped Afro and old enough to have a smile with deep crinkle marks at the corners, stood at the front of the room, surveying the kids who came through the door. The blue-eyed girl came in and took the first empty seat. Through the corners of her eyes she took little sneaking looks around the room. *She's scared, too,* Maggie thought. Maggie studied the woman, who was obviously Mrs. Hardison, and felt hopeful for the first time. She looked as though she might be nice. Maybe she—

Maggie was jostled as two large boys fought for the remaining empty seat in the back row. A hand gripped her shoulder and a voice said, "Move it."

She looked up at a tall boy who was standing close to her. "I said, 'Move it,' " he repeated. "You got my seat."

His friend laughed, and the boy said to Maggie, "Hurry up, girl."

"This is my seat," she said.

"Not for long." He pushed at her shoulder.

She stared up at him. "Let go of me."

"Listen, fatso—"

That did it. Maggie clenched her right fist and shot it with all her strength into the boy's stomach.

"Whoooeee!" his friend yelled as the boy backed off so fast that he fell over the seat behind him.

Some of the kids around her laughed. She heard one of the boys yell, "Hey, man! You see what that little chubby girl just did to old Jerico?"

Mrs. Hardison suddenly appeared in the aisle in front of Maggie. She wasn't smiling now as she looked down at Maggie. The bell in the hall rang so loudly that Maggie wanted to hold her hands over her ears. As soon as the clanging died away, Mrs. Hardison asked, "Would you like to tell me what happened?"

Maggie groaned and wished she could slide under the desk. She had wanted everything to go right this time. She had really wanted to stay out of any kind of trouble at school, just to prove to Grandma that she could do it. And here she was mixed up in a big mess, even before classes had begun!

# 2

"I hit him," Maggie said.

"Yeah!" Jerico had scrambled to his feet. He had a pained look on his face as he rubbed his stomach. "Carter there saw it. He could tell you what she did to me. That girl is mean. She coulda killed me."

Some of the kids laughed again, but Mrs. Hardison didn't even smile. "Are you hurt, Jerico?"

Jerico seemed to think for a minute. "Yeah. I think I am. Maybe I ought to go home."

Carter hooted. "You gotta go to the nurse's office first, and she never goin' to send you home! She seen you try enough before."

Mrs. Hardison looked at Maggie. "Have you anything to say about this?"

"No, ma'am," Maggie said.

"Your name is—?"

"Margaret—Maggie Ledoux."

"So you accept the blame, Maggie?"

Maggie nodded. She picked up her handbag and notebook, ready to make the trek to the principal's office, but a voice suddenly spoke out.

"It wasn't her fault, Mrs. Hardison. He was pushing at her. I saw him. He tried to shove her out of her seat."

Maggie stared at the blue-eyed girl, who was half standing, half kneeling on her seat. Her eyes seemed even larger because she looked so frightened.

"Is that right, Maggie?" Mrs. Hardison asked.

"Yes."

Mrs. Hardison turned to Jerico, who smiled at her and said, "Hey, no big deal. I think I'm not sick anymore."

"Just in the head," someone yelled, and the boys hooted and laughed again.

"Then please take the empty seat over by my desk," Mrs. Hardison told Jerico. "I'll talk to you and Maggie after class." She walked to the front of the room and quickly brought the class to order. The blue-eyed girl turned around before Maggie could react. She hoped she'd get a chance after class to thank her.

Everyone was assigned a locker and given a combination for the lock. "Keep those combinations to yourself," Mrs. Hardison announced.

But Carter mumbled, "Those lockers no harder to open than a cracker box."

The rest of the morning was filled with information about everything from how to get an absence excuse to how to use the school library. Printed sheets listing school clubs and activities were handed out.

"I'll give you a few minutes to check the ones in which you're interested," Mrs. Hardison said. "Sign your name and homeroom number at the top, and we'll collect them when you've finished."

Maggie glanced down the list. She wasn't interested in joining anything. She wanted to walk back to Grandma's house after school and curl up on the window seat in Grandma's cozy little library and munch an apple and read a good book. What were all these things? Student council? Camera club? Drama club? Cheerettes? Yuck!

"You haven't checked anything, Maggie."

Maggie jumped, startled to find Mrs. Hardison standing behind her. "I—I don't see anything I like to do."

"How about one of the teams? Do you like any kind of sports?"

"No."

"Not any? How about basketball?"

"I hate basketball."

"She too stuck up to play basketball," Carter said. "Look at her in that prissy stuck-up dress, like some movie star."

"Movie stars gotta be pretty," Jerico said. "No movie star gonna be fat, like her."

A couple of the kids in the room snickered.

Maggie knew she wasn't fat. With just twelve pounds to lose she might still be a little bit plump, but she wasn't fat. And she wasn't going to let Jerico or Carter or anyone else know how much that remark had hurt. She sat up as straight as she could and smoothed out the skirt of her dress, desperately wishing she had worn jeans. "As a matter of fact," she said to Mrs. Hardison, "I think I'll sign up for the drama club."

Mrs. Hardison smiled and gave Maggie's shoulder a little pat as she left to walk up the aisle, looking over shoulders at other papers.

The bell rang as the papers were being collected. Maggie tried to squeeze through the aisle toward the blue-eyed girl, but the girl was through the door before Maggie could reach her.

Maggie went to the back of the room, waiting by Mrs. Hardison's desk while the room cleared.

"Jerico!" Mrs. Hardison said, and the lanky boy, who was already halfway through the door, stopped.

He turned and smiled. "Hey! Almost forgot," he said and ambled back to the desk.

"I don't think we need to go through what happened or didn't happen again," Mrs. Hardison said to Maggie and Jerico. "I think we just need to remember that there *are* rules of behavior, and we *are* going to keep them."

"Well we expect *you* to," Jerico said. "You're the teacher."

"Jerico?"

"Okay. Okay. But how come you talkin' to me and not her? She's the one with the mean fist."

"I'm talking to both of you."

"But you lookin' at me."

"Maggie?"

"I understand," Maggie said. "I'm sorry I hit him."

Mrs. Hardison smiled. "All right. We'll forget it happened. Run along, both of you. I'll see you bright and early tomorrow morning."

Jerico bounded up the aisle and out of the room. Maggie picked up her notebook and followed reluctantly, wondering if Jerico and his friend, Carter, would be waiting in the hall.

She opened the door cautiously and stepped into the almost empty hallway. Its tiled floors, scuffed by many shoes, gleamed only around the edges. Jerico and Carter were standing a few feet away, heads bent together as they talked.

"Maggie?"

The blue-eyed girl was pressed so tightly against the wall that she seemed to be holding it in place. Maggie smiled, delighted to see her. The girl glanced toward Jerico and back to Maggie. "I thought you might want somebody with you until you got out of the building."

"Thanks," Maggie said. "I'm awfully glad to see you! I—" She stopped. "I don't know your name."

"Lisa. Lisa Toler."

"I wanted to talk to you."

"I didn't know if you did or not."

Maggie fished the scrap of paper with her locker number out of her handbag. "I'd like to find my locker. I might as well leave my notebook here."

"Mine is over on this side of the hall. Maybe yours is near it."

It was. Maggie found it right away, put her notebook inside, and closed it, spinning the lock.

They started toward the stairway. Carter didn't look at them as they passed, but Jerico grinned. It seemed like a friendly grin, but for some reason it frightened Maggie. She pretended she didn't see it.

"Do you walk home?" Maggie asked. "Or do you take the bus?"

"I walk. We're renting a house over on Salisbury."

"Really? I have to cross Salisbury to get to my grand-mother's house on Devonshire."

"Then your grandmother's house must be just a block from ours! Do you stay with her after school?"

They clip-clopped down the stairs and hurried past the rows of trophy cases toward the main doors of the school. The floors of the old building were ornate with black-and-white patterns of tile, echoing the hollow sounds of their footsteps, and the large dark doors of the auditorium loomed to their left. Maggie was glad when they pushed open the outside doors, even though the August air hit them like the heat from an open oven door. Buses were lined up at the curb, some of them pulling away into traffic. Between and around them were lines of automobiles, mothers peering from behind the wheels, looking for their children.

Maggie shifted her handbag into her other arm and said, "Some things are kind of hard to talk about."

"You don't have to tell me anything."

"But I want to. I really wanted to tell you when we were in the counselor's office, but I didn't know how. I live with my grandmother."

"Oh."

Maggie hurried to explain. "I don't have a mother. She died when I was two years old. And my father just got married again."

"Is he on his honeymoon?"

"Sort of. They're making a movie in Italy. At least, my father is. He's a director."

Lisa stopped and stared at Maggie. "You're kidding. Right?"

"I wish I were kidding. I wish a lot of things. I wish I knew my mother. I wish I were skinny." She watched Lisa's eyes grow bigger and bigger. "Hey, I even wish I had blue eyes, too!"

Lisa giggled. Then she asked, "Is that really true about your father?"

"Really."

"Is your new mother a movie star?"

"She's not my mother!" Maggie kicked at a twig near her foot and began to walk. Lisa hurried to catch up with her. "Her name is Kiki Dillon, and she's only twenty years old, and I've never met her," Maggie said.

The light changed at Westheimer, and the girls ran across the street.

"This is exciting!" Lisa said.

Maggie turned from the bins of fruit and vegetables crowded against the sidewalk at the small corner market. "It's not exciting to me," she said solemnly. "It's horrible."

They walked silently for half a block before Lisa said, "I'm sorry. I wouldn't like it if my father got married again either. What I meant was that *you're* exciting."

"Me?"

"Yes. Because you're interesting and different. What I mean is that you seem to like looking pretty and don't think that you have to look just like everybody else. And you're awfully brave. It really was brave of you to sock that big Jerico in the stomach."

Maggie and Lisa looked at each other for a moment, then began to giggle.

"What's so funny?" Maggie managed to ask.

"I don't know," Lisa said, and they laughed so hard that they bent double, holding their stomachs.

An old lady, with food stains on her faded dress and a small hat pulled over her forehead and ears, stopped to stare at them. "Laughter will help cure the world of its ills," she said.

"Yes, ma'am," Maggie answered politely.

She and Lisa ran down the street toward Kirby, bursts of laughter floating behind them like popping soap bubbles.

By the time they crossed Kirby, they were out of breath.

Maggie, panting, leaned against a lamppost. "You were brave, too," she managed to say. "You stood up for me, and you even waited for me in the hall."

Lisa let out a long breath. "Jerico scares me."

"Don't be afraid of Jerico."

"What if he's mad at us? He got in trouble because of us. What if he tries to get even?"

"He won't. Forget about him," Maggie said. "He's probably already forgotten about us."

The girls walked on, toward Salisbury. They didn't laugh now. They didn't even talk much. Maggie wondered if Lisa were right. Should they be afraid of Jerico and what he might do?

## 3

Maggie got home before Grandma did. She pulled the mail out of the box and sorted through it before she unlocked the front door. Nothing from her father. Oh well, she didn't care. He never had been much of a letter writer, so why should he change now?

The house was cool and quiet, almost too quiet. Maggie tossed the mail on the hall table and wished that Lisa had invited her to come in or that she had asked Lisa to come with her to Grandma's house. But she and Lisa had stood on the corner at Salisbury and stared at each other as though they'd run out of things to talk about and finally said they'd see each other tomorrow.

Maggie realized that she didn't know anything about Lisa. She wondered if Lisa had a real family with brothers or sisters and if she liked to eat apples and read mystery stories. She wondered what New Jersey was like and what kind of work Lisa's father did and why he had to move all the way to Houston to find a job. She made a peanut-butter sandwich for lunch and settled down in the library with the mystery novel Grandma had bought her, careful to lick the peanut butter off her fingers before she turned each page.

Soon Maggie was inside the story, shivering with the characters, who were trapped inside a house, wondering if someone else was in the house with them, hiding from them. The lights suddenly went out. They waited, wondering, listening. The doorknob slowly turned.

"Maggie?"

With a yelp Maggie leaped to her feet, throwing the book into the air.

"I didn't mean to frighten you!" Grandma poked her head into the doorway. "Didn't you hear me come in?"

Maggie sighed loudly and flopped onto the window seat. "I didn't hear anything. You know how it is when you're into a good book."

Grandma laughed and sat in the big armchair. "Unfortunately, I do. I've even missed telephone calls." She leaned forward eagerly. "But tell me. I've been eager all day to find out. How did things go at school?"

"Okay," Maggie said.

"Just okay?"

Maggie shrugged.

"I know nothing much could go on in just half a day, but I thought you might meet someone you'd like to have for a friend."

"Well," Maggie said, "I talked to a girl named Lisa, who lives on Salisbury. We walked partway home together."

Grandma beamed. "Would you like to invite her over tomorrow?"

"I don't know her telephone number."

"When you see her at school, you can ask."

"Grandma! I just met her. We aren't really friends. Not yet, anyway."

"Sorry," Grandma said. "I want you to like living here in Houston. I guess I'm pushing."

"I guess you are," Maggie said. She giggled.

Grandma changed the subject. "Who's your homeroom teacher?"

"Mrs. Hardison. So far she's nice."

"I don't know her. Hmmm, I thought you might get into Julia Underson's class. She's a friend of mine."

"I wouldn't want to be in your friend's class, Grandma."

"You're right. That could be sticky. Well, did you sign up for any clubs?"

Maggie nodded. "Drama club."

"Oh?" Grandma looked surprised. "Why, Maggie, how nice. You'll love Mrs. Finch. She's the drama coach. Would you believe she taught your mother when she went to Greely? She gave her so much encouragement. She even went to all the high school productions your mother was in. I remember when the high school put on *The Sound of Music* and your mother played Maria."

Maggie tried to picture her mother as a high school student, but she could see only the laughing girl in the snapshots. She wished she had known her mother.

"I didn't know you were interested in acting," Grandma said.

"I'm not," Maggie said.

"But you signed up for the drama club."

"I had to sign up for something."

Grandma looked at Maggie as though she were trying to see inside the jumble of thoughts behind her words. "Did everything go well today, Maggie?"

Maggie stood up and stretched. "Usually, Grandma, the only questions I get asked about school are, 'How are your grades?' and 'Have you been in any trouble?'"

Grandma got up and put an arm around Maggie's shoulders. "Well then, to make you feel more at home, how are your grades, and have you been in any trouble?"

"I know a better question," Maggie said. "Why don't you ask, 'Are you hungry?'"

"That *is* a better question. I'm going to make barbecued chicken for dinner. Why don't you put together a tossed salad?"

They walked to the kitchen, arms around each other. Mrs. Hardison had said, "We'll forget about what happened today," so that made it all right for Maggie to forget. She was awfully glad that Grandma didn't have to know about what she did to Jerico.

In the morning Grandma dropped Maggie off again in front of the school. "Have a lovely, wonderful day!" she said, and leaned over to kiss Maggie's cheek.

For a few moments Maggie clung to her grandmother. Once again she had that horrible fear of being alone. But Grandma said, "Say 'hi' to Lisa for me."

"You're not very subtle, Grandma," Maggie said. She sat up straight, tugged at her jeans, picked up her handbag, and climbed out of the car.

"It worked, didn't it?" Grandma yelled as Maggie was shutting the door.

Maggie laughed and waved good-bye. She wished Grandma didn't have a job, and she wished she could just stay home with Grandma. She wished there wasn't any such thing as school, and—

"Hi."

Maggie turned to see Lisa standing beside her. She was surprised at how glad she was to see her.

"What's the matter?" Lisa asked. "Did I scare you?"

Maggie giggled. "Just surprised me."

"We got our phone in yesterday," Lisa said. "If you want, we could trade telephone numbers."

"Okay," Maggie said.

"Maybe you could come over on Saturday."

"Sure. And you might like to come to my house, too. My uncle Dennis will probably be there. He brings his ice-cream freezer and makes homemade ice cream."

"He must be a good cook."

"He's a terrible cook. He just cooks stuff out of the frozen-food section. The only things he knows how to make are spaghetti and ice cream, which he says are all that's important."

"You have the most interesting family," Lisa said.

A first bell rang, and they joined the kids who were pouring through the wide front doors of the school.

"Tell me about your family," Maggie said.

Lisa sighed. "They're just a family, that's all. I've got a mother, a father, a brother who's eight, and a sister who's six. See. Nothing exciting."

Maggie wondered what it would be like to have a brother or a sister. She thought about the cousins who visited during the summer. They were fun to have around, but sometimes they got in the way. Would it be the same with brothers and sisters?

They had just reached the second floor when Maggie was poked in the back so hard that she stumbled and almost fell. She turned to see Jerico and Carter behind her.

"Oh, pardon me!" Jerico said. "It sure gets crowded in here. Everybody bumpin' into everybody else all the time." He and Carter laughed.

Maggie didn't say anything to them, and neither did Lisa. Maggie stepped aside, and Lisa followed her. She hoped the boys would go on to their homeroom, but instead they tagged after the girls.

"I have to get my notebook out of my locker," Maggie said to Lisa, and she stopped as soon as she found her number.

"The floor's all wet here," Lisa said. "It looks like someone mopped it."

Jerico and Carter stood aside and watched as Maggie tried to open her locker. She was in such a hurry that she went past the combination twice. Her fingers felt big and fumbly, and she wished she could yell at them to go away. She took a deep breath and finally pulled open the door of her locker.

Her notebook lay there in a puddle of water.

"Oh, no!" She heard Lisa gasp.

Maggie picked up the notebook and held it out. Water ran from it. Part of the cover came off in her hand, and she could see it was ruined.

"Well, my, my, my," Carter said. "Just look at that!"

"Some people got bad luck," Jerico said. He and Carter laughed.

Maggie didn't stop to think. Furiously, she grabbed the notebook in both hands and swung it at Jerico, hitting him in the shoulder. Before Carter could jump back, she had socked him with it, too.

"You rotten, slimy nerds!" she yelled at them.

Jerico and Carter yelled back. People began crowding around them. She pulled the notebook up to swing again.

"What's this? What's going on here?"

Strong hands pulled her back so suddenly that she dropped the notebook. She found herself whirled around so that she was looking up at a tall man with gray hair and a moustache.

"The principal," she heard someone murmur. "It's Mr. Enery!"

"M—my notebook," Maggie managed to stammer. "They poured water in my locker! They ruined—"

The principal interrupted. His face was as stern and set as the stone faces carved into Mt. Rushmore. "I don't know why you're blaming those boys for the water in your locker," he said. "A pipe broke in the building last night. We plan to make an announcement in the homerooms this morning.

Only a few lockers were affected. Apparently yours was one of them."

"Oh! I didn't know! I thought—"

"Come to the office with me, please," Mr. Enery said. "I'm going to want to speak to your parents. We're not going to tolerate this kind of behavior in our school!"

# 4

"May I come, too?" Lisa's voice was so frightened that it wobbled like a broken bicycle wheel. "Maybe I could help explain."

"I don't think explanations are necessary," Mr. Enery said.

"Hey there, Mr. Enery, you ain't heard it all." Jerico loped up to the principal and smiled. "Carter and me, we been devilin' that girl. Just like to see her get mad like a little puffed chicken. Why, we thought it was real funny when she tried to hit us."

"From what I could see, she did hit you."

"She hit you, Carter? You look all right to me."

"Look at her," Carter said. "She not good enough to hit nothin'. They throw her off the baseball team every time she get up to bat."

"You're telling me this was all in fun?" Mr. Enery asked.

"Sure," Jerico said. "We just clowning around before the bell ring. School ain't even started yet, so we just havin' fun."

He looked down at Maggie. Everyone else in the hall was looking at Maggie. She could see Mrs. Hardison standing behind some of the kids. Maggie wanted to cry. She wanted to run out of this place and back to Grandma's house and throw herself on her bed with the soft comforter and cry until all these people disappeared.

Instead she looked up at Mr. Enery, took a deep breath to steady herself, and said, "I lost my temper."

Jerico hooted. "See how funny she bein' right now? Look at the way she make her round little chin wobble!"

The bell rang, clearing the hall of spectators as quickly as though a magician had waved a wand over it. Mrs. Hardison edged forward, wincing against the blast of sound. As soon as the clanging stopped, she said to Mr. Enery, "I think there are mitigating circumstances here."

"Is this young lady in your homeroom?"

"Yes. And so are the boys. If it's all right with you, I'd like to handle the situation."

He sighed loudly. "Gladly. This is only the first day of school. I was hoping everything would run smoothly."

Mr. Enery strode down the hall toward his office, but Mrs. Hardison folded her arms across her chest and studied each· of them in turn. "I've got a class to take care of," she finally said. "So this is no time to talk about your behavior. Come back to my room after school, so we can discuss what happened."

Without waiting for an answer, she turned and walked quickly toward her classroom. As they followed, Maggie said to Jerico, "I'm sorry I hit you."

Jerico smiled broadly. "You go down to Mr. Enery's office and he call your mother, that's bad news for you."

"I got that idea. You and Carter were nice to help me out. Thanks."

"Nobody ever call Carter and me nice. We don't ever be nice. We just don't want that anybody take you out of the game so soon. We like to handle things our own way."

Maggie heard Lisa take a sharp breath. She shivered,

wondering if it was a blast from the air conditioner that was making her suddenly cold. "What do you mean?" she asked Jerico. "What are you talking about?"

Carter leaned over Jerico's shoulder. "Never mind," he said. "You gonna find out soon enough!"

"Yeah," Jerico said. "Soon as we think up somethin' good." He held his hands like claws and made a mad-monster laugh in the back of his throat.

Mrs. Hardison held open the door of the classroom and stood aside for them to enter. "Jerico!" she said sharply.

Jerico grabbed his throat. "You hear that awful noise, Mrs. Hardison? I think somethin' I ate for breakfast must of not agreed with me."

"Listen to me," Maggie mumbled to Jerico as they went toward the nearest empty seats. "I don't want to be in any more trouble."

"Girl," he said, "you don't got a choice!"

The next few hours were so busy that Maggie didn't have time to think about Jerico. There were new teachers to meet, textbooks to collect, notes to take, and every so often there was an announcement over the intercom. Finally, just before the eleven o'clock bell the intercom crackled, and a voice announced that time had been reserved before lunch for the extracurricular activity clubs to meet, and a long list of room numbers was read.

Drama. Maggie had almost forgotten that she had signed up for the drama club. Well, just like everything else today, it was one more thing to do and get over with. Dutifully, she went to the room assigned to the drama club meeting.

It was a large room, empty in the center, with chairs around the edge, and the teacher's desk at the back, near the windows. Some theater posters of Broadway plays were framed and hanging on one wall. A couple of kids were talking, heads together in one corner. Maggie avoided that corner and plopped into a chair at the side wall. Why did she sign up for the drama club? That was dumb. She didn't want to be here, and they wouldn't want her. She had never been in a play at any of the boarding schools. She didn't know the first thing about drama and didn't care to know.

The door opened and a group of kids shoved through. They seemed to know the kids in the corner and hurried over to them. In the doorway, behind them, stood someone looking as lonely as Maggie felt. Lisa!

Lisa spotted Maggie, brightened as though someone had turned on a light in her head, and sighed loudly, as though her life had suddenly been spared.

"I didn't know you had signed up for drama!" they said in unison as Lisa rushed over to take the chair next to Maggie's. She collapsed into it, giggling.

"We could be a Greek chorus," Maggie said.

"I didn't know you were interested in drama," Lisa said.

"I didn't know, either," Maggie told her. "I had to sign up for something, so I picked this." She decided not to explain about Jerico's mean remark and how she had reacted to it.

Lisa leaned back in her chair, resting her head against one of the posters. "Didn't you ever think about being a movie star? I have."

"I wouldn't want to be a movie star. They never get to just go to a movie or to the beach without people staring at them or trying to get their autograph. That wouldn't be any fun."

"Sure it would! It would be wonderful to have so much attention! If I could—" Lisa stopped, blinked, and said, "Oh, I forgot. Your father's a director. You've probably met a lot of movie stars."

"Not many," Maggie said. "Just enough to know I wouldn't want to be one."

"Well, when I'm a movie star," Lisa said, "you'll be the first person I'll give my autograph to."

"I'll frame it."

A tiny woman, no taller than Maggie, bounced into the room. Her short gray hair was a mass of curls that looked like little springs, and she rocked up and down on her toes as she surveyed the kids in the classroom, giving Maggie the feeling that at any moment the woman would leap into the air.

"Good morning," she said in a voice that seemed too large for her, and she smiled and bowed to them, as though she were on stage. "I'm Mrs. Clara Finch, the drama club adviser at Greely Middle School."

She paused, and the kids who seemed to know each other said together, "Good morning, Mrs. Finch."

"I've enjoyed working with some of you," she said, "but there are a few new faces here. It's time for all of us to get acquainted." She looked at Maggie. "We'll begin with you, young lady. Will you please tell us your name and a little something about yourself?"

"My name is Maggie Le—"

Mrs. Finch gave an especially energetic bounce on her toes and swept her arms upward. "On your feet, my dear! Stand tall, hold your head up, and speak out!"

Maggie awkwardly managed to stand and said loudly, "My name is Maggie Ledoux. I moved to Houston this summer."

Mrs. Finch cocked her head to one side like a little bird and said, "We must have met before, Maggie. You look so familiar."

"No." Maggie shook her head. "This is the first time we've met."

She began to sit down again, but Mrs. Finch waved her

arms grandly and said, "Wait, Maggie. Tell us something about your dramatic experience."

"I haven't any," Maggie said, feeling more uncomfortable than ever.

"You have never been on a stage?"

"Never."

Mrs. Finch smiled. "You are lovely, raw material, Maggie. You have a fine speaking voice, and it wouldn't surprise me to learn that you sing well. It will be a pleasure to have you in the drama club." She looked at Lisa. "What beautiful blue eyes!" she said. "Young lady, will you please stand and take your turn in telling us about yourself?"

Maggie dropped back into her chair, somewhat stunned, feeling as pleased as though she'd been tapped by the Good Fairy. She'd never met any teacher quite like Mrs. Finch.

Lisa was standing now, and Maggie could see she was trying hard to do what Mrs. Finch had said. Lisa's back was straight, and she was speaking loudly and clearly.

"—and we just moved to Houston a few weeks ago," she said. "When I was in the sixth grade, I was in the Christmas pageant and in the graduating class play, and when I was in the fifth grade, I had the part of Pocahontas in the historical pageant, and when I was younger—well, I always liked to be in plays and to sing, and when I'm ready for high school, I want to go to the High School for the Performing Arts and be in their drama department, and someday—" Lisa suddenly stopped, ducked her head, and shrugged.

Mrs. Finch beamed at Lisa and finished the sentence for her as though it had been planned. "And someday, acting may be your career choice."

She went on to the next student and the next. Most of them had been in school plays. A couple had even been in community theater productions. But Maggie felt as comfortable as though she were inside a hug. Hadn't Mrs. Finch told her that she was lovely raw material?

When everyone had had a turn, Mrs. Finch clasped her hands and said, "I think it's important for us to know each other and to know about each other because any dramatic production demands teamwork. We'll need to work as a team, supporting, caring, doing our best—no matter what our roles— to make sure the production is successful. We'll meet after classes on Mondays, but when we're in rehearsal, we'll have to spend extra time working. Do you all understand this?"

Maggie nodded. She saw the other heads bobbing up and down, too.

Mrs. Finch began to tell them some interesting, behind-the-scenes stories about Broadway theater productions, stories that made them all laugh.

The bell for lunch rang so suddenly that Maggie jumped. How did the hour go by so fast? She picked up her books and stood up just as Lisa did. They smiled at each other. "This is going to be great!" Lisa said. "I like her."

"I do, too," Maggie said.

"She's so interesting that for a while I even forgot about Jerico."

"Jerico?"

"Maggie! How could you forget what Jerico said? We have to be prepared. We don't know what he might do to you!"

# 5

During the next few weeks Maggie thought often about what Mrs. Finch said about teamwork. In a way, she felt as though she and Lisa had formed a team. They walked home from school together, ate Uncle Dennis's vanilla ice cream, played with Lisa's little sister, put on a birthday party for Grandma's next-door neighbor, Annie Sue, who had a third birthday, and spent hours and hours reading parts in the scripts Mrs. Finch had let them check out. And Mrs. Finch had been right. Maggie found she could sing. When Mrs. Finch showed her how to take deep breaths all the way down to her abdomen and how to bounce the notes off the roof of her mouth, Maggie's voice rang out clearly.

Lisa had a strong voice, too, so they tried out all the Broadway show tunes they knew, dancing across Lisa's kitchen like the orphans in *Annie*, waving mops and singing, "The Hard-knock Life," and hanging over the landing on Grandma's stairway to belt out, "Don't Cry for Me, Argentina."

Jerico and Carter still teased and insulted Maggie and sometimes talked with their heads together, stopping to look at her and smile wickedly, but Maggie didn't worry about them now. She was sure their threats were just talk. That first day after school, when Mrs. Hardison had met with them, she had simply told them they were all to stay away from each other and Maggie was to try to control her temper. This was the last warning.

Maggie understood. Apparently, the boys did, too. School still wasn't much better than it had ever been, but Lisa and the drama club made up for all the rest.

On the last Saturday in September Lisa had to go shopping with her mother, so Maggie leaned her elbows on the counter in the kitchen and watched Grandma slice carrots.

"There isn't anything to do," Maggie said.

Grandma turned from the sink. "Would you like to cut up these carrots for me?"

"I'd like to make brownies. Or maybe go to the movies. Or maybe—"

"I think you're bored because Lisa isn't here. I'm glad you found such a nice friend."

Maggie thought a moment. "I guess we are friends. It's just kind of scary to think about our being friends."

Grandma put down the knife and wiped her hands on her terry-cloth apron. "Why should it be scary?"

"Oh, you know, because people move away. Or they make friends with other people. Or—oh, there are lots of reasons."

"Yes, sometimes people get hurt," Grandma said. "But if you're so afraid of losing that you can't give, then your life is going to be very dull—as boring as it is right now."

"Grandma, I didn't mean I was bored." Maggie tried to explain, afraid that her grandmother's feelings would be hurt.

But Grandma laughed and came around the counter to hug Maggie. "Cutting up carrots is not my idea of fun and excitement, either," she said. "Maybe we could go to an early movie."

The doorbell rang, and Grandma looked at her watch. "Mail must be here," she said, and went to the door.

Maggie grabbed one of the carrot pieces and stuck it in her mouth, munching it as she carefully began to cut the others in small pieces.

"Here's a letter from your father," Grandma said as she returned to the kitchen.

Maggie dried her hands and took the letter from her grandmother. She opened it with a paring knife, careful not to cut into the Italian stamp. She had been saving all the foreign stamps on his letters. Most were from Italy, but a couple of his letters had been mailed from Switzerland, one from Austria, and one from Paris.

"Another delay, I guess," Maggie said.

"You haven't even opened it," Grandma told her.

"But every letter is the same. It's always some problem. The film was supposed to be completed three months ago."

She read the letter. It wasn't very long. It was really just a note. Her father's words were written with such jubilance that they seemed to sparkle on the page.

"Listen, Grandma," Maggie said, and she read aloud, " 'We're ready to return to the States now, and I'm pleased— so very, very pleased with the end result of all our hard work. This film will be a classic. I'm sure of it. We had our production problems, but right now they don't seem to matter, because my feeling is that it's all been worthwhile. More than worthwhile! Great! Fantastic! (Not much modesty here, is there, darling?)

" 'Maggie, this means we'll be seeing you very soon. It won't be on the way home from Italy, as I had originally planned, because I want to be on hand for the final cutting. It's too important not to stay on top of it all. So we'll fly directly to L.A., and by the end of October—the middle of November, at the latest—we'll come to Houston just to see you, to spend some unhurried, leisurely time with you. Kiki is especially eager to meet you.'"

Maggie put down the letter and sighed. "Then he says some stuff about missing me. That's it."

"He does miss you, honey," Grandma said.

"He's not coming when he said he would."

"But he tells you his reason, and it's a good one."

"Well, at least it puts off having to meet Kiki." Maggie carefully folded the letter and put it back into the envelope. "Maybe I'll graduate from high school, and I still won't have met Kiki. Maybe I'll graduate from college, and I still won't—"

Grandma took Maggie's hands and whirled her around and around the kitchen. "And maybe you'll be married with fourteen noisy children and be fifty years old, and you still won't have met Kiki."

"Grandma! Be serious!" But Maggie couldn't keep from laughing.

"When you do meet her," Grandma said, "you might like her very much."

"No, I won't!" Maggie said.

The front door banged open and Dennis called, "Here comes the ice-cream maker! Who wants creamy vanilla ice cream?"

Grandma and Maggie looked at each other. Grandma's eyes twinkled, and Maggie giggled. "We want chocolate!" they yelled together.

Dennis poked his head into the kitchen. He looked bewildered. In an aggrieved voice he asked, "Why would you want chocolate? What's wrong with vanilla?"

Maggie and Grandma laughed so hard that they couldn't answer.

"It's all right for Maggie to act like she's twelve," Dennis said, "but, Momma, you're not acting your age."

"Yes, I am," Grandma said. "I'm in my second childhood."

"The house seems too quiet. Usually someone is hanging over the landing, singing at the top of her lungs." Dennis looked around the room. "Where's the other superstar?"

"She had to go shopping with her mother," Maggie answered.

Dennis put the ice-cream freezer on the counter. "When are we going to see you in a play?" he asked.

Maggie shrugged. "I saw Mrs. Finch in the hall yesterday. She said she had a surprise for the drama club. She'd tell us about it on Monday." Maggie looked at her grandmother. "She told me again she was sure we'd met before. Isn't that funny?"

"Remember? I said she was your mother's drama teacher when your mother went to Greely."

"But—"

"And the first time I laid eyes on you, I told you how much you looked like your mother. Mrs. Finch is seeing Jeanne in you." Grandma smiled. "She'd be surprised if you told her who you are."

"I don't think I want her to know," Maggie said.

Grandma nodded. "Jeanne was very fond of Mrs. Finch. Did I ever tell you about the bouquet of carnations Mrs. Finch sent to Jeanne when she was in *The Sound of Music?*"

"Tell me about it," Maggie said, and she forgot all about Mrs. Finch's surprise until the drama class met after school on Monday afternoon.

Mrs. Finch was especially bouncy. Maggie suppressed a giggle as she thought how funny it would be if Mrs. Finch gave a gigantic bounce and flew right out the window.

"We're going to have auditions for a musical to be put

on by our nearby high school." Mrs. Finch's words popped out like tiny explosions. "We've been asked to fill the parts of Kurt and Brigitta, so two of our students will appear in their production of *The Sound of Music.*"

"Oh!" Maggie gasped, then clapped her hands over her mouth. The very same musical her mother had been in!

Mrs. Finch's eyes sparkled as she smiled at her. "Excited, are you, Maggie? Well, you'll be glad to know that you're one of the girls I have in mind who might be acceptable for the part of Brigitta. You and Jo Beth and Yolanda and Lisa. Now, for Kurt's part, I think Tim and Pete and Allen ought to try out."

Maggie and Lisa glanced at each other. Lisa's eyes were wider than ever, and Maggie knew how much she wanted the part. But Maggie wanted it, too. It would be exciting to perform in the same musical in which her mother had performed. It wouldn't be the same part, but it would be the same play. Grandma would love it. Dennis would come. Maybe even her aunts Janet and Sharon and their families would come to Houston to see it.

But Lisa wanted to win the part, and Lisa was her friend.

"Maggie?" Mrs. Finch was staring at her. "No time for daydreaming. Go to the desk and get a copy of the script."

Lisa was standing by the desk, clutching her script against her chest with both hands. Maggie picked up another copy of the script, looked at it, then back at Lisa.

"Good luck," she said to Lisa.

Lisa nodded. "You're supposed to say, 'Break a leg.'"

"I don't think you say that until after you get the part, and not until you're ready to go on stage."

"Okay then. Good luck." Lisa hugged her script even tighter and tried to smile. "I'm wishing you luck, Maggie, but I want that part."

"So do I," Maggie said.

She sat down and opened the script, ready to study the lines, but the words didn't come into focus. What would happen if she won the role instead of Lisa? Maggie wondered how badly she really did want that part.

6

Mrs. Finch asked those she had chosen to audition to mark special pages in their scripts and study them. She took the boys first. She had picked three of the smallest boys in the class for the part of Kurt. Mrs. Finch had them read aloud over and over again.

Finally, she stood up and walked over to Allen. "What's the matter?" she asked. "I know you can read better than this. You don't seem to be trying."

Allen shrugged. "I don't want the part. Those kids in the movie were too goody-goody. I thought it was a five-finger gag."

"Since you feel that way, you may leave," Mrs. Finch said. As Allen scrambled to pick up his books, she turned to the other two. "You'd both do a fine job as Kurt. It's going to be hard to choose, so I won't try to do it right now. Just to be safe, please check with your parents and make sure you'll be able to attend rehearsals."

"Rehearsals? Oh-oh," Tim said.

Mrs. Finch sighed. "Of course there will be rehearsals. They're scheduled for six weeks, every day after school from four-thirty to a quarter of seven, and they begin Wednesday, the day after tomorrow."

"But I've got soccer some of those times."

Mrs. Finch just shrugged and smiled at Pete. "Would you like to play Kurt?"

"Yeah!" Pete shouted. "I would! And I can come to rehearsals. No problem."

"Fine!" Mrs. Finch turned to the four girls who had been alternating between studying their scripts and checking to see how the boys were handling their audition. "Let's start with Jo Beth," she said.

Jo Beth walked slowly to the front of the room, pausing while the boys grabbed their books and raced outside.

Maggie was so nervous that her fingers stuck damply to the pages of the script. She listened to Jo Beth read her lines, thinking that Jo Beth wasn't very good. She guessed it was mean, but somehow it made her feel better. If she got up and stammered through her lines, she'd at least feel she wasn't the only one who goofed it. Yolanda was okay. Maybe she would get it. But Lisa was next, and Lisa was so perfect that Maggie decided that the rest of them didn't have a chance. Maggie was a little disappointed because she would have loved to have been in the same musical her mother had been in. But if Lisa were the best, then obviously Mrs. Finch was going to choose her. Maggie stopped worrying and began to relax.

She thought about the actress in the movie who played Brigitta. Lisa was playing it the same way—as a follower, a little quiet, a little demure. But the actress wasn't anything like Maggie, and Maggie felt uncomfortable trying to be like her. Since the part was going to Lisa anyway, Maggie decided she'd have fun with the role and do it her own way, giving Brigitta a touch of mischief.

When it was her turn, she did. She even made Mrs. Finch laugh.

"Well," Mrs. Finch said, "that's a slightly unusual interpretation of Brigitta, but quite effective." She looked at her watch. "We've got time to go over these scripts again."

Yolanda stood up. "Mrs. Finch, I don't think I can go to all those rehearsals. I take ballet lessons on Tuesdays and Thursdays, and I can't miss or my ballet teacher has a screaming fit."

"I'm sorry, Yolanda," Mrs. Finch said. "If you got the part, you would absolutely have to attend every rehearsal you were called for."

Yolanda picked up her books. "I guess I'm out then."

As she walked out of the door, Jo Beth climbed from her chair. "I'll make it easier for you," she said. "I know I'm not as good as Lisa or Maggie."

Mrs. Finch held up a hand. "We don't make rash decisions after just one reading, Jo Beth. Let's work on the script for a while. I'd like to help you get a feel for it."

Jo Beth shook her head. "I think I'm too tall anyway. What if the high school girls who are going to play Liesl and Louisa are shorter than I am? That would look terrible. So I'd rather try out for something else later."

Mrs. Finch thought a moment. "I think I have exactly the part in mind for you. It's something you'll love."

"What?"

"In November we're going to produce a review of songs and skits from Broadway musicals, right here at Greely. I'll tell you about it later." Mrs. Finch turned to Maggie and Lisa. "As far as transportation goes, I can drive you to the high school on my way home each afternoon, and I'm sure you can find someone who can take you home after rehearsals. But are there any problems in attending rehearsals? Any reason why either of you couldn't take this part?" Both girls shook their heads, so Mrs. Finch said, "All right then, let's get to work."

But at four-thirty she shook her head. "It's very difficult to choose between you. I'm going to have to sleep on it. I may even ask you to read again. Come and see me after classes tomorrow."

"You mean we'll have to wait a whole day to find out?" Lisa asked. "I don't think I can stand it!"

Mrs. Finch rocked back and forth on her toes. "Professional actresses have to wait much longer than one day to hear audition results."

Lisa's cheeks grew suddenly pink, and she ducked her head. "I want to be an actress, so I guess waiting is something I'll have to get used to."

Mrs. Finch smiled and made a shooing motion with her hands. "Run along, girls. I'll see you tomorrow."

As they walked toward their homes, Maggie and Lisa talked about the teachers and kids at school, the awful desserts in the school cafeteria, even an old movie they'd seen on television. They didn't want to talk about the script. They couldn't. What would they say?

When they reached the corner at Salisbury, Lisa hugged her books to her chest and said, "It's kind of close to dinner time. I'd better see if I can help my mother do anything."

"Sure," Maggie said. She thought about their plans. "What about algebra? Do you still want to come over and do homework together?"

"Maybe tomorrow," Lisa said, and Maggie understood. Until Mrs. Finch decided which one of them would have that part in *The Sound of Music*, it was uncomfortable being together.

"See you tomorrow," Maggie said, and went on toward Grandma's house.

Everything seemed even more strained the next day. Maggie had thought about that part. She had even dreamed about it. She had been standing on top of a mountain. She had opened her mouth to sing, and a group of people who had been watching her turned and bolted, running away down the valley. She had called to them to come back and promised not to sing to them anymore, but they didn't pay attention to her. Soon they had gone, and in her dream it made her very sad.

"I had the strangest dream," she said to Lisa when she saw her before the first bell rang, and she told her, trying to make it sound funny.

But Lisa didn't laugh. She just hunched her shoulders a little and said, "Dreams are supposed to be symbolic. My mother's reading a book about dreams. They all mean something."

"But that was a weird dream. What could it mean?"

"I don't know," Lisa said. "My mother said you're supposed to ask your dream what it means. Why don't you do that?"

"Ask a dream? That sounds crazy." But during the day Maggie thought about what Lisa said. It was after lunch in history class, when she was feeling warm and full and just a little bit drowsy, that she stopped paying attention to the dull report that Brian Carey was reading and let her dream slide back into her mind. She could see the mountain, the meadow, the scene right out of *The Sound of Music*. And she saw herself begin to sing and the people turn and run.

"What do you mean?" she asked her dream.

One of the people in the meadow stopped and looked at her sadly before running on. It was Lisa.

"Oh!" Maggie said, and shot upright against her desk.

Brian stopped reading his report. Everyone stared at her.

43

"Sorry," she mumbled, and slumped back in her seat. Brian glared at her and went on reading.

*Dreams aren't true*, she told herself. It didn't mean that if she got the part instead of Lisa, that she would lose Lisa for a friend. What could a dream know?

But the unhappiness of the dream stayed with her during the rest of the afternoon, and she was nervous when she met Lisa outside the door of Mrs. Finch's classroom.

"Lisa," she began, "I—that is, whoever gets the part— well, it doesn't matter, does it? I mean that I—I don't want us not to be friends."

When she said the word, the sound of it surprised her. Friends. Lisa was the first real friend she had ever had.

Lisa smiled. "Of course we'll still be friends."

Maggie sighed with relief. "Then let's go inside and find out the news!"

Mrs. Finch was sitting next to a slender, slightly balding man whose smile was so wide that it made his eyes scrunch up. "This is Mr. Cassidy," she said. "He's the drama coach who'll be directing *The Sound of Music*. Since I couldn't make up my mind between you, I'm going to let him do it."

He motioned them to chairs, then leaned forward and talked to them about the play, trying to put them at ease. He had them read, then sing a little.

"Sing what?" Maggie asked.

"Anything," he said. "I just want to hear your singing voices."

They sang and they read again and again. The longer they worked, the harder Lisa seemed to try. Her voice became strained at one point, and Mr. Cassidy helped her to take deep breaths and do a relaxing exercise. But the work had the opposite effect on Maggie, whose tension disappeared. She was having fun. Maybe because it was interesting being somebody else for a change. She was almost disappointed when Mr. Cassidy said, "That should do it, girls. You're both wonderful."

They stared at him, waiting for what would come next. He leaned over his chair, huddling with Mrs. Finch. Maggie couldn't hear a word they were saying. She looked at Lisa, who just stared at her with wide eyes.

Finally, Mr. Cassidy stood up and smiled again. "As I said, you're both talented, and I wish I had parts for you both, but I don't. So I've had to make a difficult choice. I'm casting Maggie in the part."

Maggie yelped and jumped up and down, hugging Lisa, who hugged her back. "I can't wait to tell Grandma!" she shouted.

"Congratulations," Lisa said. She was smiling, but her eyes looked kind of funny, as though she was trying not to cry.

"Oh, Lisa," Maggie murmured, "I know you wanted it, too."

"No problem." Lisa took a step backward. "We couldn't both have it. You'll do a great job."

"Thanks," Maggie said. She felt a tiny bit guilty, but the excitement of being chosen was so strong that the guilt vanished as fast as the last cookie on a plate, and Maggie jumped up and down again, laughing.

Mr. Cassidy grinned at her. "Before you dash off," he said, "let's go over a few last-minute instructions."

Maggie followed him over to the desk, where he handed her a rehearsal schedule, a flier for the program, and some printed instructions. She tried to pay attention to what he was saying, but all she could think was, "Wait until I tell Grandma that I'm going to be in the same play my mother was in!"

Finally Mr. Cassidy said, "Tomorrow, when you're a little calmer and can pay attention, Mrs. Finch will go over everything with you again. Right now you can go home and tell your family the good news."

"Thank you," Maggie said. "Thank you! Thank you!" She swooped up her books, only dropping them twice, and managed to rush through the doorway.

The hallway was empty.

"Lisa?" she asked, but of course Lisa wasn't there to answer.

Maggie ran down the stairs and out the front door. Maybe Lisa would have waited for her outside. But apparently Lisa had already gone home.

A sharp, cold kind of sick feeling hit Maggie right in the middle of her stomach.

"Hey, come on." Maggie spoke aloud, hoping to believe what she was saying. "Lisa knew I wouldn't be out of there for a while, and she probably had to get home."

"You talkin' to us?"

Maggie whirled to see Jerico and Carter on the steps behind her.

"What you doin' hangin' around school so late? You get yourself in trouble again?" Jerico asked.

"No," Maggie said as the excitement rushed back. "I got a part in the high school play."

"See, I told you she was a movie-star type," Carter said. "She gettin' more stuck up by the minute."

There was a strange sparkle in Jerico's eyes as he said, "You like gettin' up on a stage in front of everybody, do you?"

"You listen to me," Maggie said. "Don't you dare try to spoil this for me! Or—or—"

"Or what?" Jerico laughed. "You goin' to sock me in the stomach again?"

Maggie didn't answer. She turned and ran toward Grandma's house as fast as she could go.

# 7

Grandma jumped up and down, too, when Maggie told her the news. "Call Sharon and Janet!" she said. "And by that time Dennis will be home from his office, and you can call and tell him! We'll celebrate!"

"I'm going to write to Dad," Maggie said. She looked at the flier. "The show will be on the last two weekends in October. I want him to come and see me—it."

"We'll all be there," Grandma said. "And as far as we're concerned, you'll be the star."

"Oh, Grandma," Maggie said, "Brigitta isn't a very big part. Don't you remember the movie?"

"Yes, I do." Grandma's eyes twinkled. "What puzzles me is how they'll manage to get those Alps on stage in that little auditorium."

Maggie laughed and hugged Grandma again. "I've never been in a play. Never in my whole life."

"I'm glad it's *The Sound of Music*," Grandma said. "It's like a circle coming around again. First your mother, now you."

"I'm kind of scared, too."

"It's not being really *scared* scared," Grandma said. "It's a kind of nervous excitement. Jeanne said it made for a better performance." She held Maggie at arms' length. "Go call your aunts! Now! And as soon as you've told them the good news, let's have dinner at that hamburger place where they've got all those bowls of yummy stuff you can spread on your hamburgers. You can invite Lisa to go with us if you'd like."

"Lisa?" The strange feeling came back again.

Grandma nodded. "It would be fun to have Lisa with us." She didn't say anything else, but Maggie knew that she understood.

Grandma left the kitchen. Sharon's and Janet's and Dennis's telephone numbers were listed on the little bulletin board over the phone. She'd go down the list. But with her hand on the receiver Maggie hesitated. No, she'd call Lisa first.

Lisa's mother answered. Behind her was the sound of music blaring and a loud argument going on between Lisa's little brother and sister.

"Be quiet!" Mrs. Toler said. "Oh, I don't mean you, Maggie. Congratulations! Lisa told me—will you please turn down the stereo, and stop that argument! I'm on the telephone. I know you're so pleased, Maggie. I told you to stop, and I mean it. One—two— Here comes Lisa. I'll turn you over to her, Maggie."

The background noise ceased abruptly, and Lisa's voice said, "Hi."

"Hi," Maggie said, and told Lisa about Grandma's plan. "I hope you can come with us," she added, and as she waited for Lisa's answer, she kept thinking, *Please say yes! Please!*

"Just a minute," Lisa said, and she yelled at the top of her lungs, "Mama, can I have dinner with Maggie and her grandma?"

Maggie heard Mrs. Toler yell, "That's a good idea," and Lisa said, "Sure. Right now?"

The strange pain slid away with Maggie's loud sigh of relief, and the giddy feeling of happy excitement rushed back. "In about half an hour," she said. "Okay?"

"Okay," Lisa said. "I'll be at your house by then."

Maggie called her aunts, who both promised to come to Houston to see the play, and Dennis, who said he was going to be sure to catch the ten o'clock newscast on channel two because this was a really important item and bound to be their lead story.

The doorbell rang just as Maggie hung up the telephone. She rushed to the door, sure that it was Lisa. But instead, there stood Gloria, from next door, with Annie Sue and Bonnie Joy.

"Hi," Gloria said, stepping inside as the little girls rushed to grab Maggie around the legs.

"Oh, my goodness, I forgot!" Grandma said as she came into the hallway. "I did promise to baby-sit, didn't I?"

"I hope it's still all right," Gloria said. "My friend got tickets to the rock concert at the Summit, and I been thinkin' about how much I want to go ever since he asked me."

"Well, of course I'll baby-sit," Grandma said. "Could we take them with us to get hamburgers?"

"Sure. They like hamburgers."

"We're celebrating," Grandma said. "Maggie won a part in the high school play, *The Sound of Music*."

"Well, think of that! Someday you might be a movie star, just like your mama was." Gloria beamed at Maggie, who beamed right back, delighted to be compared to the beautiful mother she couldn't remember. Gloria added, "I bet lots of famous stars got started in high school plays. I recollect Blinky Parker."

For a moment no one said anything. Then Maggie said, "I never heard of Blinky Parker."

"That don't surprise me," Gloria said. "He was a couple

of years ahead of me in high school. He got the big role in the high school musical that year—*Dames at Sea*—and he probably could have been a big star someday, 'cept that he never did nothin' else with actin', and after graduation he went to work in a gas station."

"But you said—"

"That's right," Gloria said. "But you won't be like Blinky Parker, and I'll be back for the kids right after the concert's over. Just watch out for Bonnie Joy. I've got her out of diapers now, but she can't always be trusted."

Lisa arrived as Gloria was leaving, and in a short while they all joined the crowd getting hamburgers.

During dinner Annie Sue spilled her glass of milk on Grandma, and Bonnie Joy managed to dump her hamburger, cheese sauce and all, in Maggie's lap. But for some reason everything seemed funny, and the french fries were even better than Maggie remembered, so they all had a wonderful time.

Later, just before she went to bed, Maggie stood in front of the portrait of her mother. "I'm going to be in the same play that you were in," she said. She wished her mother could be here. She imagined that she'd be as happy as Grandma was when she told her the news.

There was one more person left to tell. Maggie pulled her box of stationery from the desk drawer and began a letter to her father. She told him about winning the part in the audition, then wrote, "It's the very same play Mother was in when she was in high school, so it means a lot to me. I know it's not a big part, but I'm still exicted about it, and I hope you can come to Houston while the play is on, so you can see it. You said you might be able to come to Houston near the end of October, and the play will be on the last two weekends in October. So please come, Daddy! Please!"

It wasn't until after she had climbed into bed, pulling

the quilt up to her chin, that she realized all during the evening no one had mentioned the play.

And during the next day before school it was the same. Lisa didn't talk about Maggie's part in the play, so neither did Maggie. The fact was there, as obvious as the statue of General Sam Houston in Hermann Park, but they were pretending it wasn't or that it was invisible. Maggie didn't know what else to do, but she would have loved to tell Lisa how scared she was and how much she wanted her father to come to the play and how her mother had been Maria in the very same play when she was in high school, but she couldn't.

The first bell rang, and she and Lisa went upstairs to their homeroom. Lisa was ahead of her, and when Maggie tried to follow, Jerico attempted to squeeze through the doorway at the same time. Maggie accidentally stepped on his toes.

"Ouch!" Jerico moaned loudly and hopped on one foot, following her to her desk. He leaned over it and said in a low voice, "You did that on purpose."

"You were pushing me. I couldn't help it."

"Oh, my, my, you gonna be so sorry you stomp on my toes on purpose. Here you be workin' hard to be a big star over at the high school and don't even know that all the same time Carter and me is plannin' a surprise for you! And now, 'cause you stomp on my toes, that surprise is goin' to be even better."

"What are you going to do?"

"We don't know yet. We givin' it lots of thought."

"Just remember—I warned you," Maggie mumbled as the second bell rang and Jerico ambled back to his desk.

The day seemed to drag. Maggie could hardly wait until after school. She said good-bye to Lisa and tried not to run as she hurried to Mrs. Finch's room.

Mrs. Finch already had her handbag and car keys in

hand. Pete was standing beside her. "Ready?" she asked, and Maggie nodded, so nervous that she couldn't speak.

Mrs. Finch chattered to Maggie and Pete as they drove the six blocks to the high school, which was a large, gray square building. She didn't seem to notice that Maggie didn't say a word. She drove into the parking lot and up to a side door. "Just go in there and follow the hallway. You'll come to the theater. It's in the middle of the building. They even have a marquee."

"What's a marquee?"

"A lighted sign. It looks like a real theater. You both have rides home?"

"My mom's coming for me," Pete said as he hopped out of the car.

"My grandmother will be here," Maggie said. She stopped to take a deep breath, then began to slide across the seat, but Mrs. Finch rested a hand on Maggie's arm.

"Don't feel intimidated, Maggie. The young people you'll meet were all in middle school just a couple of years ago. You'll find they're nice kids. Just relax, work hard, and enjoy being in the production."

Maggie managed a smile. She went into the building, fighting the urge to run after Mrs. Finch's car, shouting, "I want to go home!"

Many of the high school students had left the school for the day, but she could hear voices and laughter ahead, down the hallway, so she followed the sound. That's probably where Pete had gone. She found herself in an open space, and just as Mrs. Finch had said, there were signs with lights around them above the doors to the auditorium.

No one paid attention to Maggie. A woman arrived with two little girls, and Maggie smiled at them, but they didn't smile back.

*Why do I do things like this to myself?* Maggie thought,

and she wondered if her mother had ever felt the same way. She put her books on the floor against the wall, then wished she had kept them just to hang onto.

"Yeah, here comes Alex!" one of the high school girls shouted, and Maggie watched a tall, broad-shouldered boy stride into the room. He had dark hair, almost the color of her own, and he walked briskly with his head up as though he knew he was as handsome as everyone thought he was but didn't care.

"Don't call him Alex. You've got to call him 'Captain Von Trapp' now." A tall, beautiful girl with long blond hair looked at him from under her lashes and laughed.

Alex smiled at everyone, including Maggie—who gulped when his eyes met hers—and made an elaborate bow. He took the blond girl's left hand, looked into her eyes, and began to sing, "They say that falling in love is wonderful . . . "

The girl put a hand over his mouth. "Wrong song, wrong play. That was last year's."

"I'm warming up. Besides, I don't know the words to the songs in this one yet."

She laughed. "Then don't show off to me. Go sing to someone else."

Alex turned and saw Maggie watching him. "Okay," he said. "Here's a beautiful girl. I'll sing to her." Before Maggie realized what was happening, Alex had taken both of her hands and was singing the love song to her.

# 8

His eyes were deep and dark, and Maggie imagined she could see herself reflected in them. She was like a statue, unable to move, almost unable to breathe, and she could feel her cheeks burning. What if everyone started laughing at her?

But no one laughed, and she heard Mr. Cassidy shout, "That's enough, Alex. Settle down. We've got work to do."

Alex stopped singing and smiled at Maggie. "Hi," he said. "I'm Alex Bradley. I bet you're going to be Brigitta, one of my daughters." He tilted his head, as though he were studying her and added, "I do have good-looking daughters."

"Everybody over here," Mr. Cassidy called.

"What's your name?" Alex asked Maggie.

"M-Maggie L-Le-Ledoux." Maggie winced, wondering if he would tease her for stammering, but Alex just led her into the group.

"I'd like you to meet Maggie Ledoux," he said. "She'll be Brigitta." He let go of Maggie's hand and turned to the two little girls. "And you must be my youngest children, Marta and Gretl." Just as politely he introduced himself to them.

"Is he always like that?" she heard a girl behind her whisper.

And another girl giggled before she murmured back, "Yeah. Everybody loves Alex. He's a real character." There was a pause and she added, "But don't ever get in his car with him. He drives like a fool."

"How come?"

"I don't know. That's just the way Alex is."

Maggie had never met anyone like Alex, and she found it hard to stop looking at him, even when Mr. Cassidy announced, "Let's get down to business." He introduced everyone, then began to give instructions.

He showed them the theater, the makeup room, and the dressing rooms. The high school kids seemed to feel at home in their theater, but Maggie was awed by the huge stage and the rows and rows of seats. They'd be filled with people who'd be watching her, staring at her. Maggie took a step backward, bumping into someone who put a hand on her shoulder to steady her.

"It scared the poop out of me," she heard Alex say. "I was a freshman, and it was my first real part, and all I could think about was eyes down there that would be staring up at me."

Maggie shivered.

"But then it was opening night, and I was on stage, and I found out that it wasn't so bad. The audience was there because they wanted to like the play and the actors. In a way, they were cheering us on. And I liked the audience and the applause. I found I could make them laugh. It must have gone to my head because that's what I want to do the rest of my life."

"You're going to be an actor?"

"That's right. I'll graduate in May, and I've already got an application in for a very special dramatic academy in New

York. I'm keeping my fingers crossed." He smiled and added, "If you have any extra fingers, you might keep them crossed for me, too."

"I will!" Maggie said.

"Better cross them that he'll make his grades." The beautiful blond girl, whom Maggie had found was named Kate and was going to play the lead part of Maria, grabbed Alex's arm.

"Don't bring up grades," Alex said. "Why should an actor worry about meaningless things like grades?"

"They're not meaningless if they keep you from getting accepted at the drama academy."

"Alex! Kate! Pay attention!" Mr. Cassidy called.

"Come on," Kate said. "We're supposed to form into groups and start read-throughs."

"Maggie," someone called. "Over here."

For the rest of the afternoon Maggie's attention was on the words in the script. She was surprised when Mr. Cassidy announced, "It's six forty-five, everybody. Let's break. See you tomorrow."

"Anyone need a ride home?" Alex asked.

"Whooo! You think we're crazy?" Dodi, the stocky, cheerful Mother Abbess, called. "We want to stay alive."

"I'm a careful driver," Alex said. "I know what I'm doing."

"So do we," someone called. "See you tomorrow."

Maggie found her books and tucked her script in with them. She followed the others out to the parking lot and saw Grandma's car parked in the first row.

Alex loped past her and the others, and she saw him jump into a low, red sports car. With a screech of tires he backed it, turned, and the car bounced out of the driveway.

She hurried to Grandma's car and climbed in, flinging her books into the back and flopping against the seat.

Grandma grinned at her. "Hard work, was it?"

Maggie sighed. "It was hard, but fun."

"Tell me about it." Grandma started the car and steered it into line, leaving the parking lot and heading toward Westheimer.

"There's so much to tell, I don't know just where to start. First of all I met Alex, and then Mr. Cassidy introduced everybody to everybody else, and he showed us around the theater part of the school, and Alex told me how scared he was the first time he was on stage, but that it turned out all right, and we broke into groups and did a read-through." She leaned back and sighed loudly.

"All of that in one breath?" Grandma laughed.

"That was it," Maggie said.

"You mentioned someone named Alex, but you didn't tell me who Alex is."

"He's Alex Bradley, and he's a senior, and he's very handsome, and he wants to go to New York to study and become an actor, and he's awfully nice, and one of the high school girls said that everybody loves Alex."

"He must be quite special."

Maggie slid down a little further in her seat, hugging her arms across her chest. "I guess."

Grandma seemed to be concentrating on traffic, and Maggie was glad she didn't ask any more questions about Alex. There was lots more she could tell Grandma, but she didn't want to. She wanted to keep some of it to herself. She thought about how he had sung to her and asked her name and how he had seemed to know how scared she was and wanted to make things right for her. She had never met anybody in her whole life like Alex.

As she parked the car in the garage, Grandma said, "Dinner's in the oven and will be on the table in two minutes. And while you're in rehearsal, I'll take care of the dishes. You'll need to get right to your homework after dinner."

"That's not fair to you," Maggie protested.

"Sure it is," Grandma said. "You can do the dishes on weekends. Everything will come out even."

But time didn't come out even. It was ten-fifteen before Maggie finished the last of her homework. It was too late to call Lisa. Oh well, she'd tell her about everything in the morning. Maggie took a quick shower, climbed into bed, and fell asleep thinking of Alex Bradley's handsome face.

Maggie waited at the top of the brick steps leading to the front doors of Greely, watching intently for Lisa. As she saw Lisa hop out of her father's car, she ran down the stairs to meet her.

"Hi," Lisa said. "How did it go?"

"It was hard work," Maggie said.

They turned toward the school, walking slowly, having to step around and between the other kids who were arriving. Lisa tilted her head and examined Maggie's face. "You look kind of—um—sparkly or something."

"Well," Maggie said. "It was exciting."

"I guess so," Lisa said. "Did I tell you that my little sister talked Dad into letting us get a puppy?"

"When?"

"He said maybe for Christmas."

"Oh."

"I don't know what kind of dog he'll let us get. I'd like a big one, maybe a German shepherd."

They reached the main doors. In a couple of minutes the bell would ring. "Lisa," Maggie said.

"What?"

"My mother was in *The Sound of Music* when she was in high school. Now I'm in the same play. Grandma said it was like a circle coming around."

"You didn't tell me that."

"I know."

Lisa paused and took a deep breath. "Maggie, I'm glad you got the part. I wanted it, but— I am glad. Really."

"Thanks."

Lisa smiled. "Tell me what you did."

"We saw everything in the theater and did our first read-through of the script."

"Were the high school kids nice?"

Maggie nodded. "They were okay. Especially Alex."

"Who's Alex?"

"He's a senior. He plays the Captain. He—uh—he sang to me."

"I thought he was supposed to sing to Maria."

"Not in the script. He just wanted to sing to someone, so he sang to me."

"He sounds like a show-off."

"Oh, no!" Maggie said. "He's wonderful!"

Lisa giggled. "Maggie, your cheeks are getting pink."

Maggie put a hand to her face. "Because it's hot out here. That's why."

"I thought maybe because you liked him."

Maggie tried to sound noncommittal. "Everybody likes him."

"Then he's probably conceited. Anyhow, if he's a senior, he wouldn't be interested in a twelve-year-old girl."

"I'm almost thirteen!" Maggie snapped.

But the bell rang, drowning out her words. The doors flew open as people pushed into the hall. Lisa was ahead of her, going toward the stairs. Maggie followed, wishing that Lisa had understood what she had been trying to tell her about Alex.

Maggie shrugged. How could she expect Lisa to understand when she didn't understand it herself?

9

It wasn't until nine-thirty on Monday evening that Maggie's father telephoned.

"Congratulations, Margaret! We'll see another Julie Andrews in you. Right?"

"Daddy, I don't have the same part that Julie Andrews had. I'm just one of the Captain's children. I'm Brigitta."

"Wasn't she the littlest one?"

"No. That was Gretl."

"Well, whatever, Kiki and I are proud of you. Just a minute." Maggie heard a woman's voice in the background, and Roger said, "Kiki told me to tell you to break a leg. You know what that means, don't you?"

"Yes, Daddy. Are you going to come to Houston to see me in the play?"

"Kiki and I are certainly going to do our best."

"But you said your work on the film should be finished around that time."

"That's something I can't count on, Margaret. We work with a schedule, but ninety-nine times out of a hundred, a film runs over schedule."

"Do you work on weekends, too? The play's only going to be on during two weekends. One is going to be the last weekend in October. You could come just for a weekend."

"Margaret, you know I'd rather see you in your play than anything else in the world."

Maggie clenched her jaw, poking it into the end of the receiver as though her father was standing there. "Then come."

He chuckled. "All right, Margaret. Last weekend in October. Better send me the exact dates, and I'll get my secretary to put it on the calendar."

Maggie spoke softly. "One of them is my birthday."

"Your birthday! Of course! You don't think I'd forget, do you? We'll all celebrate! We'll invite your grandmother and some of your friends to go out to dinner after the play. How's that?"

"That would be great."

There was a pause, and Maggie's father asked, "How is school going this time, Margaret?"

"Fine."

"I assume that you or your grandmother would inform me if there were any problems."

Maggie groaned. She couldn't blame her father for expecting problems because she'd created enough of them in the past, but she wished he hadn't brought it up.

"Why don't you just trust me?" she asked. "Why expect something bad to happen?"

"I was just—"

"How would you like it if I said, "Hi, Daddy. What have you been doing wrong lately?"

"Margaret, don't raise your voice."

"I'm sorry."

"And please don't get that sullen attitude." He sighed. "We do seem to have trouble communicating, don't we?"

Maggie felt tears burning behind her eyes. "I really am sorry, Daddy," she said. "I don't want us to be angry with each other. I want you to come to the play."

"Just a minute, Margaret. What? Oh, all right. Kiki is reminding me that we have a dinner engagement. I'll have to say good night."

"I'll see you in October, Daddy."

"Right. I love you, Margaret."

"I love you, too, Daddy."

"Kiki says to tell you she sends her love."

"Good-bye, Daddy. Thanks for calling." Maggie hung up the receiver and stared at it. He would come. He would. He said he would come, didn't he? Okay. She'd believe him.

She found Grandma in the den watching her favorite private-eye program.

"That man is gorgeous," Grandma said.

Maggie sat on the sofa next to her grandmother and watched the dark-haired man on the screen. "Alex is even better looking," she said.

"I can't wait to see this Alex," Grandma told her. "After rehearsal tomorrow why don't you point him out to me?"

"I think you've seen him. He's got long legs, and he always moves fast, and he gets in his little red sports car and takes off in a hurry."

"Good gracious!" Grandma said. "I have seen him!" She shook her head. "I wonder what problems he's trying to run away from."

Maggie turned and stared at Grandma. "What are you talking about?"

"The way he drives. I think it's a symptom. He may be racing to get away from something that's making him un-happy and not know why he's doing it."

"But he always acts like he's happy."

"Maybe he's learned how to cover up his feelings."

Maggie felt as though she needed to come to Alex's defense. "Grandma, how could you know so much about him? You've never met him. All we were talking about was that he's good looking."

"He certainly is," Grandma said. "I agree."

"And he's funny and nice and friendly to everybody."

"I like him already," Grandma said.

Maggie waited until a commercial came on. Then she asked, "How much older than you was Grandpa?"

"A little over four years."

"Daddy is an awful lot older than Kiki." Maggie peered at her grandmother from the corners of her eyes. Grandma was calmly watching the television screen. "I mean if Alex went to New York and studied for a few years and then worked hard getting started as an actor and was so busy he didn't have time to fall in love with anyone and get married, well, I'd be a lot older, too." She suddenly found herself blurting out, "Grandma, how old does a person have to be to fall in love?"

As soon as Maggie had said the words, she groaned with embarrassment and wished she could grab them out of the air and stuff them back in her throat and maybe strangle on them. But Grandma just said, "Oh, I don't know. There really aren't any rules. I remember when I first fell madly in love. I was eight."

"Eight? But you were just a little kid!"

"I know. My father was in a car pool, and one of the men was a fireman, named Don. He had flaming red hair, and I thought he was the handsomest thing I'd ever met, and I fell in love with him."

"That wasn't Grandpa!"

"No, he wasn't. Don, the fireman, became engaged that year and was married. I cried for a couple of days and refused to go to the wedding because I was so sure that he'd wait for me to grow up."

"But he was lots older than you. Alex is just six years older than me. That's not so much."

"At your age it's something of a barrier," Grandma said, "but you're right. When you're both in your twenties, it wouldn't be a problem at all."

Maggie grabbed her grandmother's hand. "Then what should I do?"

"Right now, just be a good friend to Alex. For one thing, real love is based on friendship. And for another thing, since Alex is being just a good friend to you, I think he'd be very uncomfortable if he thought that you were in love with him."

"Maybe he'll want to know someday."

Grandma squeezed her hand and smiled.

The screen showed a station break, and Maggie said, "Oh, no! I made you miss the end of your program."

"You're more interesting than any television program," Grandma said. She flipped off the set. "Time for bed."

Maggie followed her grandmother up the stairs, watching as she turned off the downstairs lights, the bottom of the stairway dissolving into a dark pool. "That was my father on the telephone," she said. "He's coming to see me in the play the last weekend in October."

"Wonderful!" Grandma said.

"He really will. He promised," Maggie said. "And he's going to take us all out to dinner to celebrate the play and my birthday."

"Good," Grandma said. "I love celebration dinners. It's the only good excuse to really pig out."

Maggie laughed and hugged her grandmother. She couldn't wait for tomorrow's rehearsal when she'd see Alex again.

———

By now she was as familiar with the high school as she was with Greely Middle School. She waved to the kids who were gathering in the theater for rehearsal and stopped to talk to the little girl who was playing Gretl. Alex was sitting on the edge of the stage, swinging his legs. "Hi, Maggie," he called.

She walked slowly down the aisle to stand in front of him. She remembered what Grandma had said. For now she'd be only a friend. "Hi," she said. "We're going to be rehearsing that 'Edelweiss' scene today, aren't we?"

"Yep," he said. "That's one of my favorites."

"Look what I got!" Dodi's voice rang out from the back of the theater. She came down the aisle waving a paper bag. "My brother got a whole bunch of packages of fortune cookies. He gave me some. Everybody have a fortune cookie!"

The others crowded around, laughing, reaching into the bag and reading their fortunes aloud.

"Hey, Alex, hop down here and get one," Dodi said.

"I don't want a fortune cookie to tell me what's going to happen," Alex said.

"Maybe you just don't want to know, period."

"Maybe so."

Dodi held the bag out to Maggie, who took one. Then Dodi held the bag up to Alex. "Take one," she said. "I'm not going to leave you out."

Alex took a cookie, broke it in two, and glanced at the slip of paper with his fortune printed on it.

"Read it aloud," she demanded.

"Forget it," he said, and threw it on the ground.

But Dodi was not going to be put off. She scooped up the paper and read in a loud voice, "Soon there will be a wedding in your family."

Alex mumbled, "I hope it means me."

Maggie gasped and held her breath.

But Kate sauntered over and said, "You? Getting married? Alex, you aren't even seriously dating anybody."

Alex smiled brightly. "The only people in my family are my mother and me," he said. "She's been married three times already and is talking about making it four. So—" he shrugged with arms outstretched—"I'm getting tired of new 'fathers.' If it's got to be one of us, I'd rather it was me. Okay?"

"Did you hear that, girls?" Dodi said. "Everybody who wants to marry Alex form a line over here!"

They all began kidding and laughing as Alex jumped from the stage and began hugging them in turn. But Maggie walked back to where Gretl and her mother were sitting and plopped into a chair next to them. She wondered if she were the only one who had seen the hurt behind Alex's smile.

# 10

As the days passed, some of the excitement of being in the musical dribbled away like an ice-cream bar left out in the sun. A lot of time was spent waiting to go on stage, waiting for someone who was blowing his lines, and waiting for one scene to be accepted before another was begun. Now and then Maggie was able to snatch a few minutes for homework. Yet homework still seemed to demand all her evening hours. In the mornings, Lisa's father was usually running late, and she arrived just in time for the first bell. So most days, except during lunch hour, Maggie rarely had a chance to talk with Lisa.

But one evening the telephone rang just as she and Grandma came in the door. Maggie ran to answer it.

"Maggie!" Lisa shouted. "Guess what! I've got the part of Annie!"

"Annie? What Annie? When? Where?"

"Give me a chance to tell you! Remember Mrs. Finch said we were going to put on a musical review? Well, there are two numbers from the play *Annie* in it, and I'm Annie!"

Lisa let out such a loud screech that Maggie pulled the receiver away and rubbed her ear.

"That's great!" Maggie said. "When—"

"I have to wear a red, curly wig and that funny dress Annie wears, and oh, yes—Jo Beth is going to be an Annie, too, only in *Annie Get Your Gun!* Isn't that a hoot? She'll be perfect!"

Maggie wondered why she felt so unhappy. It was the kind of feeling someone would have if everyone in the class were invited to a party and she were left out. Finally she was able to interrupt Lisa. "When is this musical review?"

"Oh, didn't I tell you? November. The middle. I forget the exact dates. Isn't it exciting?"

"It's wonderful," Maggie said.

Lisa was still shouting. "I'll let you go. I've got to learn my lines and my songs. Jo Beth's mother plays the piano. We're going to rehearse with her at her house tomorrow after school. See you, Maggie!"

"Sure," Maggie said, but Lisa had already hung up.

Grandma had come into the kitchen and was poking into the refrigerator and pulling out some broccoli spears and a head of lettuce.

"Mrs. Finch is putting on a musical review at Greely, and Lisa got the part of Annie," Maggie told her.

"Isn't that marvelous!" Grandma shut the refrigerator door and tossed the broccoli onto the counter near the sink. "I know how excited she must be! I hope you told her how happy we are for her!"

"Not exactly. Lisa was talking so much I didn't get a chance to say that." Grandma was studying her, so Maggie quickly added, "I did tell her it was wonderful."

Grandma turned back to the sink. "Would you mind setting the table, Maggie, while I take care of the broccoli?"

Maggie opened the cupboard that held the dishes, but instead of taking out two plates, she leaned against the door and said, "Grandma, I feel kind of left out." When her grandmother didn't say anything she added, "I'm glad Lisa is going to be Annie, but I want to be in the review, too."

"You wanted to be in the high school production."

"I know, but the review isn't until November, and I am in the drama club at Greely, and Mrs. Finch didn't even talk to me about having a part."

"You haven't been going to the club meetings. You've been in rehearsal."

"Oh, Grandma, don't you understand?"

"Tell me this," Grandma said. "Which one of your friends would you like to give up her part in the review for you? Surely, not Lisa."

"That's not what I mean. You make me sound so selfish."

"Maggie," Grandma said, "I'm tired. And I'm feeling impatient. Let's not talk about this now."

"I just wanted to tell you how I feel."

"Later. I asked you before. Will you please set the table?"

Maggie thumped the plates on the table and tossed on the napkins, knives, and forks. Grandma didn't understand. Nobody would understand. She had had more fun with Lisa before all this rehearsal stuff began. She wished that neither of them had joined the drama club. Why couldn't they have signed up for photography or creative writing or something like that?

For a while Maggie and Grandma ate in silence. That made Maggie even more unhappy. She sneaked a careful look at her grandmother while Grandma was looking down at her plate. Grandma really was tired. Maggie could see it in her face, so she tried to fight down her mixed-up, unhappy feelings and talk about anything else but the play. But the mood in the kitchen was as sticky as a steamy, muggy day. Maggie was glad when dinner was over.

The next morning, as usual, Grandma was already buttering toast by the time Maggie rushed into the kitchen.

"Hi," Grandma said. "I poured you some orange juice."

Maggie leaned on the counter. "Grandma," she said in a small voice, "I'm sorry about last night. I guess I was in a bad mood."

"I guess I was, too," Grandma said. She handed Maggie a plate with two pieces of golden toast and popped two more slices into the toaster. "I'm sorry I didn't want to listen to your problems. Want to talk about them now?"

Maggie saw her grandmother sneak a quick look at the wall clock. "No, thanks," Maggie said. "We'd better hurry and eat breakfast or we'll both be late for school."

Maggie barely made it to homeroom before the late bell rang. She didn't get a chance to talk to Lisa until the beginning of lunch break.

Maggie met Lisa at their usual spot and said, "Tell me more about the musical review."

But Lisa began waving to someone across the room. "C'mon," Lisa said to Maggie. "Jo Beth and Yolanda are saving us a place."

Maggie reluctantly followed Lisa, climbing over the bench at one of the tables, squeezing in between Yolanda and a girl named Kip, all of them busy talking about the parts they'd be playing in the musical review.

"You'll never guess all the people who are going to be in it!" Yolanda told Maggie. "Everybody in drama club, of course, but a lot of other people, too. Mrs. Finch has been signing up people all week."

"I didn't hear about it."

"It was in the school newspaper."

Maggie thought of her copy of the paper, still unread, still folded and tucked inside her history book to mark the place.

She opened her sack lunch and gobbled down the banana and the cheese sandwich. No one was talking to her anyway. They were all going on and on and on about their parts in the review.

Finally she said, "I'll see you later," and crawled out of the bench, trying not to poke Yolanda in the ribs.

"See you," Lisa called, and went back to her conversation with Jo Beth, not even asking Maggie where she was going.

Maggie went straight to Mrs. Finch's room. Luckily she was there, sitting behind her desk, a stack of papers in front of her.

Mrs. Finch put down the red pencil she had been marking papers with and said, "Oh, Maggie, how nice of you to come by. I've been hearing lovely things about you from Mr. Cassidy. He's so happy you were cast in *Sound of Music*."

"Oh," Maggie said. "Uh—thanks."

"Do sit down, Maggie."

Maggie slipped into the nearest chair. She looked at the stack of papers on the desk. "You're busy. I'd better not stay."

"And let me die of curiosity because I won't know why you came to see me?" She gave a little wiggle in her chair. "Nonsense. What's on your mind?"

"The musical review." Maggie took a breath and spoke quickly. "I want to be in it, too."

Mrs. Finch looked surprised. "How could you be? You're in rehearsal every day and will be until the play goes up."

"But *The Sound of Music* will be over the last week of October! Your musical review won't be until the middle of November!"

"Surely you realize that weeks of practice and rehearsal precede any production."

73

"But I could work extra hard."

Mrs. Finch frowned at her red pencil, then looked up at Maggie. "It's important for all actors to do their best with their roles. If they didn't, they would be letting down the entire company. I know, from experience, that handling one role and keeping up grades in academic subjects is a full-time job. I don't see any way for you to do your best with your present responsibilities and take on a role in our musical review."

Mrs. Finch's bounce had popped like an old balloon, so Maggie tried to explain. "I guess I miss—well, I miss doing things with my friends."

"Maggie," Mrs. Finch said, "there will be plenty of other opportunities for you to be in productions here at Greely. Next spring we may do *Tom Sawyer*, and that should be great fun."

Maggie got up. "Thanks, Mrs. Finch. I'm sorry I interrupted you." Mrs. Finch didn't understand, either. Nobody knew how she felt.

But Alex knew.

That afternoon he climbed into the seat beside her in the dimly lit back of the theater. "Hiding out, are you?" he asked.

"They're doing the convent scene with Maria. They don't need me."

"They don't need me, either. I'll hide out with you. What's the problem?"

Maggie sat upright. "What makes you think I have a problem?"

"Everybody has problems. Some of them get so bad they pop out like acne. Right now you're sitting here with such a big, squishy problem, I couldn't help noticing it."

"Ugh!" Maggie said. "That's yukky! That's sickening!" But she had to laugh.

"Want to talk about it?" Alex asked. So Maggie told him how left out she felt.

"I know what you mean," Alex said. "Any time you compete with people you have a hard time with friendships."

"I don't want to compete with Lisa!"

"You did compete when you got this role."

"But I didn't want to. I—I'd rather just be friends, the way we were."

"You had just met her. Right?"

"Well—yes."

"Okay, so friendships grow and some of them change. You're still friends, but in a different way. Think of it like this. Lisa will come and see you perform and tell you that you were the star of the show. Then you'll see her perform and tell her the same thing. And by that time the shows will be over and you'll both have the free time you used to have, and everything will be okay again."

"You make it sound easy. It's because you have so many friends."

"I have many kinds of friends. You'll find that different people are there at different times, just when you need them."

Maggie smiled at him. "Like you. Just now."

Alex took her hand and squeezed it. Maggie almost stopped breathing. "Okay now, friend?" he asked.

Maggie could only nod.

"Just think how glad you'll be to see Lisa and your family down in front cheering you on. Only a few more weeks!"

"And your family will be here, too."

Alex's smile slid away. He looked toward the stage and let go of her hand. "I only have my mom, and sometimes she's busy and doesn't come."

"Your friends will be there," Maggie said.

Alex sat up and grinned at her. "Right!" he said, and loped down the aisle toward the stage.

"I want everyone down here," Mr. Cassidy called from below center stage.

Maggie picked up her books and joined the others. "Costume fitting tomorrow," he told them. "We'll do a costume rehearsal Friday, and I've got two invitations for groups of you to perform in a couple of weeks."

"Perform where?" Maggie asked.

Kate turned to her. "We raise some money to help pay for the productions by putting on our singing acts at country clubs as entertainment for their members' luncheons."

"It's fun," Dodi said.

Alex added, "And we usually get good stuff to eat afterwards."

Mr. Cassidy said, "We'll give you a schedule next week." He made a notation on his clipboard. "I'll have to get our younger members excused from their schools for a couple of hours. One group particularly wants the 'Edelweiss' scene, which means all the children."

"Are the costumes here now?" Dodi asked.

"You're getting ahead of me," Mr. Cassidy said. "I was about to announce that the girls can go to the costume room and try on their costumes. Each one has the name of the character pinned on the shoulder."

None of the girls waited to hear what he might say next. Chattering and laughing, they ran toward the costume room.

Maggie found three dresses with Brigitta's name on them. Two were too large, but the party dress looked about right. *I've lost some weight since I was measured!* she thought.

Maggie put on the party dress and looked in the mirror. With her hair pulled back, braided maybe, she'd be Brigitta. She smiled at her reflection, thinking about what Alex had said. Lisa would come to see the play. She knew she would.

And Grandma and everyone in Grandma's family. And her father. He would be there, maybe even in the front row. And he'd be proud of her and applaud more loudly than anyone else.

She was counting on it.

## 11

"Of course I'll come to opening night!" Lisa said when Maggie asked her. "You know I'll be there! And let's get together this weekend."

But on Saturday Maggie had to go to an extra rehearsal at the high school, and on Sunday Lisa had to practice the songs with Jo Beth and her mother. The next weekend was the same.

That Sunday afternoon Grandma said, "How about a movie?" but they couldn't find one they both wanted to see.

Maggie lay on her back on the rug and stared at the ceiling. "There's lots about being in a play that is very boring," she said, "but Alex is excited about it all the time. Maybe that's because he's going to be a real actor someday." She thought a moment. "Did my mother feel like I do? Or did she feel like Alex?"

"Maybe more like Alex," Grandma said. "All Jeanne ever wanted to do was act."

"I can think of lots of other things I'd rather do."

"Like what?"

"Oh, I don't know. Just lots."

"What happened to all that initial excitement?"

"It's there sometimes. When I think about Daddy coming to see the play, then I get excited."

"He'll be so proud of you!" Grandma said. "The whole audience will be filled with very proud parents—and grand-parents—for every one of the actors in the play."

"Except for Alex," Maggie said. "He only has a mother, and he doesn't think she'll come."

Grandma thought a minute before she said, "I hope he's wrong. In any case, we'll applaud extra hard for him."

Maggie scrambled to her grandmother's chair and flung her arms around her. "He needs a grandma," she said, adding, "Oh, Grandma, when you meet Alex, you're going to like him so much!"

"I like him already," Grandma said.

Maggie leaned back on her heels and said, "Oh! I almost forgot to tell you! On Thursday some of us are going to perform for the Rolling Hills Country Club. Some of the others are going to put on a show for another club on Monday."

"I wish I could see you," Grandma said. "How am I going to wait until opening night?"

"You could join the Rolling Hills Country Club." Maggie grinned.

"I'll just work on being patient."

Maggie was so busy that being patient wasn't a problem. There seemed to be so many, many things to do to get ready to put on a musical. The actors had to get used to the sets, which had gone up, and their costumes, and Mr. Cassidy had them go over and over their scenes until they were prac-tically perfect.

Each day, the minute she burst into the door of Grand-ma's house, she searched the mail. Twice there were short notes from her father, but he didn't mention his forthcoming visit to Houston.

"He will come, won't he?" Maggie asked her grand-mother.

And Grandma answered, "He said he would."

At ten-thirty on Thursday morning, Mrs. Finch drove Maggie over to the high school, where she quickly put on one of her costumes and joined the others who were going to the country club to perform. She was so nervous that her legs wobbled, and she didn't know what to do with her trembling fingers.

"This will be the first time I've ever been on the stage," she said to Dodi, who answered, "Break a leg, kid."

And to Kate, who said, "Just relax. You'll have fun."

And to Alex, who said, "I hope you feel a little bit scared because that means you'll give a better performance. It's a tradition. We're all a little scared."

"Even you?"

"Especially me."

"But what if I goof up? What if I forget my lines or ruin everything?"

"You won't," Alex said. He paused and smiled at her. "I believe in you, Maggie."

Maggie smiled back. "Thanks. You've made me feel a lot better."

Alex looked at his watch. "Want to ride over in my car?"

Before Maggie could answer Mr. Cassidy stepped up and said, "Brigitta, Kurt, Liesl, and Fredrich will ride with Kate. Gretl and Marta will go with Gretl's mother." He read off names, some of which Maggie recognized as band members. Of course, they'd need music for their songs. There seemed to be about twenty of them going to the club.

Mr. Cassidy put a hand on Alex's arm. His voice was quiet and stern. "I expect you to drive responsibly."

Alex smiled. "Sure," he said. "Don't I always?" But as Mr. Cassidy continued to look at him, Alex suddenly became serious. "I'm careful when someone's in the car with me."

"Hurry up, Maggie!" Kate called, and Maggie rushed to catch up.

"On Monday the club gave us turkey sandwiches," Kate said as they climbed in the car. "I wonder what this club will feed us today."

"Don't talk about food!" someone yelled. "Not while my stomach is jumping around!" And everyone laughed.

At the country club a plump woman, ornamented with rows of gold chains, introduced them to the members of the audience, who were seated at tables already set for lunch.

When she first looked into all those faces, Maggie found it hard to breathe, but the music began and she moved with the others into the first song. Before long, she was enjoying being a part of the act and especially enjoying the delight on the faces of the women who were being entertained. When they finished singing their last number, "Edelweiss," a few of the women had tears on their cheeks.

Maggie felt great, and she loved the enthusiastic applause. Maybe this was why her mother had loved to perform.

The woman with the gold chains climbed on stage again and said, "Thank you, thank you, for a lovely performance. We know you have to hurry back to school now, and we're so very, very glad that you came." A couple of waiters appeared and began to put salad plates on the tables.

The woman beamed at the actors and applauded again. The older kids looked at each other. Alex shrugged and led the way outside.

"No food?" Kate asked the moment they were outside the door. "Can you believe it? We put on a show like that, and they aren't going to feed us?"

Gretl's mother had already shepherded Gretl and Marta to her car, saying over and over to them, "Weren't you darling!

Just absolutely darling!" The children turned to wave good-bye as they drove away.

"We're always given *something* to eat," Kate continued. "I'm starving."

"Hey," one of the band members said, "there's a pizza place down near the corner."

"I didn't bring any money," someone said.

"I didn't bring a lunch," someone else added. "I didn't think I'd need one."

Alex fished into the pocket of his costume. He pulled out a wallet and found two dollar bills in it. "Okay," he said. "How much money have we got among us?"

"Zilch," Kate said.

But others spoke up. "I've got fifty cents."

"I've got eighty."

Alex held out his hands while those who had brought some money with them dropped it into his hands.

He counted it and said, "Eight dollars and fifty-three cents."

The trumpet player groaned. "How much food are we going to get with that?"

"Trust me," Alex said. "And follow me to the pizza place."

There was a lunchtime crowd in the pizza place, but they found parking places and followed Alex into the restaurant. He asked the man at the door, "Are you the manager?"

"Yes," the man said. He looked at their costumes. "You kids in a play or something?"

Alex explained the situation, then held out the money. "If you'll feed us, we'll give you this eight dollars and fifty-three cents and put on the same show for your customers that we did for the women in the country club."

At first the manager looked astounded. Then he began

to chuckle. Finally he laughed out loud. "Why not?" he said, and patted Alex on the shoulder. "Kid, when you grow up, you ought to be a salesman."

The band set up near the salad bar and began the opening bars. The troupe put on their show again, with just as much enthusiasm as they had the first time. The customers cheered and applauded, and when they finished "Edelweiss," the manager blew his nose and wiped his eyes. "Find seats somewhere," he said. "Hot pizza coming right up."

This was probably the most exciting day of Maggie's whole life. And Alex was the most exciting person she had ever met. She couldn't wait to tell Grandma all about it.

But opening night turned out to be even more thrilling because earlier that day Sharon and Andy drove in from Austin, and Janet and John came from Corpus Christi with Maggie's young cousins, Jason and Debbie. At six o'clock Uncle Dennis arrived, bringing Maggie a bouquet of yellow mums and presenting it to her with a flourish.

Lisa came to Grandma's house to ride to the high school with the family. She was dressed in her best navy blue dress with red trimming and kept saying, "I'm so excited, Maggie! I can't stand it!"

Everyone was wound up as tightly as one of Jason's little cars that zoomed around the kitchen floor. Everyone kept talking at the same time.

"Did anyone see where my suitcase disappeared to?"

"What time do we leave? Aren't we supposed to be there early?"

"You are not going to leave this house, Jason, with that little wind-up car in your pocket."

"I'm not going to wind it up."

"Can I borrow a small handbag, Momma? I forgot to bring mine."

"You know you will, and it will make a terrible racket, just like it did in church last week."

"I'm hungry."

"We'll eat later, Debbie."

"I knew I should have packed my black shoes."

"Cross my heart I won't wind it up."

"No!"

"Didn't you say your father and his wife would be here, Maggie?"

"Next week. It's my birthday, too. He's coming then. He promised."

"Mama brought your birthday present. She hid it upstairs."

"Jason told! Mama, Jason told!"

"Hey, everybody! Are you ready? It's time to go!"

The doorbell rang. Lisa was closest, so she threw it open. "Oh!" she shouted.

"Margaret Ledoux?" a voice asked as they all crowded around the doorway. Maggie saw a huge basket of red roses and a delivery boy's legs underneath them.

"I'm Margaret," she said.

Uncle Dennis took the basket and lifted it to the hall table.

"I've never seen anything like it!" Sharon said. "Look at all those roses!"

Grandma pulled a card from the basket and handed it to Maggie.

Maggie knew who the basket was from. Who else would send her roses? But her fingers trembled as she opened the small white envelope and read aloud, "To the star of the family. Can't wait to see you. Love from Daddy and Kiki."

"He's coming!" she cried. "He'll see the show next week!"
"We'd better get moving, or we won't see it *this* week!"
Dennis called.

"I'm ready!" Maggie cried. For just an instant she squeezed
her eyes shut and crossed her fingers. Yes. She was ready.

# 12

Opening night was even more intoxicating than Maggie had imagined. The vibrant music and an electricity that sparked the cast made the theater crackle with excitement. "This is what my mother loved," she told herself over and over.

And after the production had ended and the applause had finally died down, Lisa hugged her and said exactly what Alex had said she would. "You were the real star of the show, Maggie! You were terrific!"

Everyone in the play congratulated everyone else. "You were marvelous!" "I loved your song!" "Fantastic!"

Alex swooped down and hugged Maggie, twirling her around. "Great performance, Maggie!" he shouted.

Maggie gasped for breath as he put her down. "This is my family," she said. "Grandma, I'd like you to meet—"

But Alex was already hugging Grandma. "Hi, Grandma," he said.

"Hi, Alex." Grandma giggled as though she were Maggie's age.

Alex shook hands with everyone else, including Lisa, who stared after him as though he were already a famous star. "Wow!" she whispered. "Don't you love working with him?"

Fortunately, Maggie didn't have to answer. Mrs. Finch flew into the group, bubbling with congratulations.

Late that night, after the celebration and the hamburgers and the excitement were over and everyone was tucked into bed, Maggie snuggled under the quilt. Debbie was already a little, snoring ball, burrowing into Maggie's side of the bed. Maggie didn't mind. Everything was perfect. Nothing could spoil all this happiness. Nothing!

But the letter from her father did. It arrived on Thursday. Maggie pulled it from the stack of Grandma's mail just as she was saying, "Daddy still hasn't told me what time their plane will arrive. He hasn't said where they'll stay. And they're supposed to be here this weekend!"

Maggie took a check from the envelope. She read the letter, wadded it into a ball, and threw it on the floor.

"What is it?" Grandma asked.

"He can't come," Maggie said. Her words were so bitter that she could taste them. "More delays. He wants to be with me more than anything else, but his responsibility is to the film." She kicked the ball of rumpled paper. "He doesn't care about me! Just about that dumb picture he made!"

Grandma didn't say anything. She just wrapped her arms around Maggie and held her tightly.

"You were there for every performance!" Maggie cried. "He doesn't want to see even one!"

"A lot of people are involved in a film," Grandma said. "If it's really good, it means more jobs for them and probably a great deal more money. Your father does have a big responsibility to them."

Maggie pulled away. "But he could still come for a weekend! Just a weekend!" She scowled at the check. "I'm supposed to buy something with that for my birthday."

Grandma shook her head. "I don't have the answers, Maggie, but I'm sure your father would come if he possibly could. Trust him." Her voice lifted as though it had gone up two floors in an elevator. "I know! You can send him a playbill and those snapshots Dennis took of you in your costumes! And when you write to thank him for his present, you can tell him all about the production. He'd like that."

"I am not going to write to him," Maggie said.

"Right now you're angry," Grandma said, "and you're hungry. Let's make dinner. You'll feel better after you've eaten dinner."

But Grandma was wrong. Maggie's hurt and anger pushed itself into a lump, settled right in the middle of her stomach, and wouldn't go away.

She thought she could talk to Lisa about it during lunch on Friday, but Lisa could only say, "That's terrible! I'm sorry, Maggie," before the lunch bench filled with some of the other girls from *Annie*, Tish and Yolanda trying to outshout each other as they sang, "The Hard-knock Life."

Maybe she could talk to Alex.

But that night Alex didn't appear until almost time to go on stage. Maggie heard Mr. Cassidy say, "Alex, this is irresponsible. It's not like you."

Alex didn't smile as he said, "What difference does it make?" before he ran to the dressing room to get into costume.

Maggie turned to Kate, who was standing beside her. "What's the matter with Alex?"

Kate put a hand on Maggie's arm. Her eyes, as she still looked in the direction Alex had gone, were sad. "He was turned down by that New York academy. His grades haven't been good enough."

"Oh, no!" Maggie said. "But his acting career—"

"He'll have to go for it some other way." Kate gave Maggie a little pat. "He's really hurting. Just be patient with him."

"I'm sorry," Maggie said. "He's got so much talent. He's such a special kind of person."

With a sweep of her Mother Abbess black robes, Dodi joined them. "You hear about Alex?" she asked. When they both nodded she said, "That's tough. Too bad some famous producer or talent agent can't come and case this show and discover Alex."

"That only happens in the movies," Kate answered. "Real life isn't that easy." She and Dodi walked toward the wings of the stage.

"Curtain in five minutes," Mr. Cassidy announced.

But Maggie was thinking so hard that she couldn't move. If only her father had come! He would have seen what Alex could do! He promised to come to Houston when everything about the film was finished. Then she could make sure that he met Alex. She'd get them together somehow. She'd work out a plan.

The girls playing the nuns were getting into place on stage as the orchestra began the overture. In a few minutes Kate—in front of the curtain—would be going into her lead song. Maggie gave a hop of excitement, and this excitement had nothing to do with the play. She'd be able to help Alex. As soon as she had a chance, she'd tell him about her father. That might make him feel a little better.

But Alex stayed to himself between acts and was the first one to leave the building after the curtain fell.

"I need to tell Alex something!" Maggie complained to Mr. Cassidy.

"You can tell him tomorrow," he said. "We'll have a cast party after the play closes. Oh—and bring your grandmother to the party, too. She ought to be honored for never missing a performance."

On the way home Maggie told Grandma what she wanted to do.

"Getting them together is fine," Grandma said, "but I don't think you should tell Alex about it in advance. It might embarrass your father."

"But if Alex knows, he might feel better."

"What if he counts on it, and your father doesn't want to see him perform? Or what if your father sees him but doesn't think Alex has enough training or talent yet?"

"I want to help Alex," Maggie said.

Grandma reached over to pat Maggie's hand. "That's what good friends are for," she said.

On Saturday night Alex was back, and so was his smile, which he wore like a mask. Maggie wondered how often that smile covered up what Alex was really thinking.

The last performance was one of the best, and after the final curtain call Mr. Cassidy congratulated each actor by name. They congratulated each other, too.

"You're a good little actress, Maggie," Alex said. "Hey, happy birthday, too. I hear you're a teenager now!"

"Oh, Alex," Maggie said, bursting with the plan she couldn't tell him, "you have so much talent! You're going to be a really famous actor someday!"

"Thanks," he said. "I need a friend like you to keep telling me that."

"I will!" Maggie said. "I'll always be your friend!" She felt her cheeks growing hot and red, but she didn't care. "Even though the play's over, we'll still be friends, won't we?"

"Sure," Alex said. "And when I'm starring on Broadway, I'll send you front-row tickets."

"Really? You won't forget?"

"I won't forget."

"Alex—will you give me your telephone number? I—I mean in case I need to call you about—um—something." After she said it, she wanted to groan. Alex wouldn't know she needed it in order to have him meet her father. He would think she was just some crazy, romantic girl who wanted to call him. Oh, why couldn't she tell him about her plan!

Alex didn't question her, and best of all he didn't laugh. He just found a scrap of paper under a nearby table and pulled a stub of pencil out of his shirt pocket. "I carry this to sign autographs with," he said. He wrote his telephone number on the paper and handed it to Maggie.

"Alex, I believe in you," she said.

For just a moment the smile slipped. "That's good," he said. "Somebody needs to."

Grandma joined them. Alex greeted her, then turned to another group.

"I didn't tell," Maggie murmured to her grandmother. "But he gave me his phone number. And when Daddy gets to Houston—" She didn't finish the sentence. Grandma knew what she meant. Maggie was sure everything would work out just right.

The next few days felt as though a monster had taken a huge bite out of them, leaving empty holes. Without the hours and hours spent on rehearsals and performances, Maggie seemed to have too much time on her hands.

Mrs. Finch asked for volunteers to work crew backstage, and Maggie was the first to sign up.

"That means you'll help write the programs and paint the backdrops and do all the things like that," Mrs. Finch said.

"I can do makeup, too," Maggie said. "I learned how from the girls at the high school."

"Fine! We'll need your special talents," Mrs. Finch said.

So Maggie was working on the musical review, but she still had to fight against that left-out feeling. The actors and the crew had such different jobs that they rarely were together. Maggie sometimes watched Jo Beth in Annie Oakley's role or Lisa doing a fantastic job as Orphan Annie and kept from feeling selfish and miserable by thinking of Alex. If only she'd hear from her father.

She did write to him about the play, as Grandma had suggested, and sent copies of the photos that Dennis had taken. And she wrote later to tell him about Greely's musical review and how it was keeping her busy.

The review was set for a Friday night. The Monday before, Mrs. Finch met Maggie as she arrived at school. "Well," she said, "I see why you wanted a part in the musical."

"You do?"

Mrs. Finch nodded. "You should have told me."

"Told you what?"

Mrs. Finch put a hand on Maggie's arm. Her smile wobbled a bit as she said, "I knew I had seen you before. I saw your mother in you. Jeanne was a dear, talented girl, and I'll never forget her."

"You mean that because of my mother—?"

Mrs. Finch didn't seem to hear Maggie. She quickly glanced at her watch, interrupting Maggie. "You know the words and music to 'The Hard-knock Life' that the orphans sing, don't you?"

"Yes."

"I think you could pick up the choreography without much trouble. Suppose we make you one of the orphans? Would you like that?"

"Sure! But you don't have to because of—"

The first bell blasted away most of Mrs. Finch's sentence. "Just be at rehearsal after school," is all that Maggie heard.

Before homeroom Maggie met Lisa. "I'm going to be one of the orphans," she said.

Lisa didn't look at Maggie. "I guess Mrs. Finch had to do something."

"Do something? You mean because she knew my mother?"

"I'm not talking about your mother. I'm talking about your being in the review," Lisa said.

Jerico had just come into the room. "Maggie, you goin' to be in that review? What part you goin' to do?"

"I'm just one of the orphans," Maggie said. She kept watching Lisa, wondering what was the matter.

"That makes everythin' perfect!" Jerico said. "Don't it, Carter?" The two of them laughed and pushed each other toward their seats.

Lisa was already sitting. Maggie leaned over her and said, "I don't know what's happening, Lisa. Why don't you tell me what's wrong?"

Lisa looked up. "Nothing's wrong. Why should it be?" She paused. "Didn't you read this morning's newspaper?"

"No," Maggie said.

"You ought to," Lisa said, and turned away from Maggie. "You're in it."

# 13

Someone had brought the clipping to school and passed it around during lunch period.

"Is your father really a famous director?" Tish asked. She handed Maggie the clipping.

The story was in the society gossip column. It mentioned that Roger Ledoux, director of what was rumored would turn out to be the Academy Award-winning movie of the year, and his wife, Kiki Dillon, soon to be playing a major role in a made-for-television movie, would visit Houston to see their daughter, Margaret Ledoux, in her junior high school musical review.

"Oh, no!" Maggie shouted. "Why did he do this to me!"

Lisa looked surprised. She stopped with her sandwich halfway to her mouth and said, "I thought you sent that to the paper."

"Of course not!" Maggie said. "His secretary sends out press releases, all that dumb stuff. And it isn't even right!"

"It is now," Jo Beth said, "since you're going to be one of the orphans."

"I won't!" Maggie said. The girls were quiet, staring at

her as she tried to rub away the tears on her cheek with the back of one hand. "There are enough orphans in that song! Nobody needs me! I'm going to find Mrs. Finch right now and tell her I won't do it!"

"Maggie—" Yolanda began, but Maggie didn't stay to listen. She ran all the way to Mrs. Finch's classroom.

The classroom was empty.

Maggie leaned against the doorframe, trying to think. She needed to talk to Grandma. Grandma didn't know about the newspaper item either.

She fished a quarter from the change in her handbag and ducked into the first-floor alcove that held the pay telephone. She remembered the number of the elementary school where Grandma worked. It didn't take long to be connected with the library. But when she heard her grandmother's "hello," Maggie had a hard time answering.

"Maggie? What's the problem?"

Grandma sounded so worried that Maggie tried to calm down and explain as well as she could.

"In this morning's newspaper?" Grandma asked. She muttered something under her breath. The only words Maggie was able to understand were, "How could—? Oh, darn!"

"He didn't even write to me about coming," Maggie complained.

She heard Grandma take a deep breath. "Let's both calm down," Grandma said. "I'm sure that he wrote to you. Often the mail is delayed. I bet you'll get a letter today."

"I don't believe it."

"Listen, Maggie," Grandma said, "your father is coming to see you. That's what you really wanted, isn't it?"

"I wanted him to come and see me in *The Sound of Music.*"

"I know." Grandma paused. "But you had another reason for wanting him to come. Remember?"

"Alex!"

"That's right. Maybe you could arrange for Alex to audition for Roger."

"Oh, Grandma! I will!"

"You can call Alex tonight."

But Maggie couldn't wait that long. She scrabbled through the bottom of her handbag, came up with two dimes and a nickel, and found the number for the high school's drama department in one of the telephone books.

Her hands shook as she heard each ring. On the fifth ring someone answered. Maggie recognized the voice.

"Kate? It's Maggie."

"Maggie!" Kate said. "Everybody here has been talking about you. Dodi brought that clipping about your father to school. Wow! You should have made him come to see our play!"

"I wanted him to," Maggie said, wishing she didn't have to explain, "but he had to finish the film he was making."

"Tell me something," Kate said. "Do you get to meet lots of movie stars? Dodi said you do."

"Sometimes."

"I can't believe what it's like!"

"It's not that great."

"But what are you doing living in Houston? Don't you have a big house in Beverly Hills and a maid and all that stuff?"

"Kate, the bell's going to ring pretty soon, and I need to talk to—"

Kate interrupted. "I'm sorry. We're all just real excited about finding out your father is a famous director, and—"

"Kate."

"Okay, Maggie. You want to talk to Mr. Cassidy, I suppose, but he's in class right now."

"No." Maggie gulped and tried to keep her voice from shaking. "I want to talk to Alex."

For a long moment Kate didn't answer. Then she said, "Alex isn't here anymore. I guess you wouldn't know. Nobody would have told you."

"Told me what?" Maggie tried not to shout.

"Well, first of all, Alex totaled his car."

"No! What—?"

"Hey, don't get upset. He wasn't hurt too much. He broke his left arm and cracked two ribs, but he's okay. Anyhow, his mother got married again and sent Alex off to live with one of his aunts for a while."

"Where?"

"In Ohio or something like that. Maybe Iowa."

"You don't have his address?"

"Mr. Cassidy has it. Alex sent him a postcard and said 'hi' to everybody. If you want it, call Mr. Cassidy back sometime when he's not in class, and he'll give it to you."

*Don't you even care that he's gone?* Maggie wanted to shout, but instead she just mumbled, "Good-bye," and hung up the receiver.

Her fingers felt like numb stumps, and her head hurt. She knew she was walking, but she wasn't sure where. It didn't matter. A bell jangled loudly, echoing down the hallway, but Maggie ignored it. She pushed open the main doors of the building and went outside, dropping to the steps, hugging her legs, pulling herself into a tight ball of misery. *He said we'd always be friends, and he didn't mean it. He didn't even tell me good-bye.* Maggie put her head down on her knees and cried.

When her sobs turned into dry shudders, Maggie raised her head and saw that someone was sitting beside her. She stared into Jerico's eyes.

"You okay now?" Jerico asked. He looked concerned.

"Why should you care?" Maggie snapped, then immediately shook her head. "I'm sorry. That was rude."

"Don't need to say you're sorry," Jerico said. "When dogs get hurt, they bite. People do sort of the same thing. You look like you really hurtin'."

"I am," Maggie said, "but I promise not to bite you."

"I didn't think you would. You just a lot of bark. An awful lot."

Maggie found a tissue in her handbag and blew her nose.

"Pretty good," Jerico said. "I give that a six."

Maggie had to smile. "Why'd you come out here?" she asked.

"I seen you from the office window. I didn't like to see you cryin' like you was doin'. Makes me feel terrible to see anybody carryin' on like they lost their best friend."

Maggie's eyes began burning again. "I did lose a friend," she said.

"Wasn't Lisa. She been lookin' all over for you."

"She was?" Maggie sat up a little straighter.

"Sure. That what was botherin' you so much?"

"No," Maggie said, and she found her words about Alex spilling over just as her tears had a few minutes before.

When she had finished, Jerico said, "That don't mean he weren't your friend. People have different friends for different times and different reasons."

"That's sort of what Alex said."

"That dude was right. If everybody hang onto every friend they ever get, they have to buy a million Christmas cards, and they talk on the phone for hours every night, and their house get stuffed with people all the time, and they go broke."

Maggie giggled. "You make it sound right."

"I wouldn't tell you all that stuff if it wasn't right."

"I miss him, though."

"Well, then, when he a big star, you go see him, and

he be glad to see you, and you be glad to see him, and maybe you be friends again."

"But I wanted to help him get to be a star."

"If he good as you say, he can help himself. If he really good, he gonna want to do things for himself. So you see it all work out that you just let him alone."

A bell rang, and Jerico said, "We both gonna be in trouble if we stay here any longer."

Maggie got to her feet. "Thanks for talking with me. I'm glad we're friends now."

Jerico took a step backward and grinned. "Just like I say, friends come and go, so don't start thinkin' you gonna get away from what Carter and me got in mind to get even with you. We finally come up with a great idea."

"If you still want to get even with me, then why did you come out here and try to help me?"

Jerico's eyes gleamed. "That was one thing. This another. What Carter and me got in mind—well, it's just too good a plan to waste."

## 14

After school Lisa found Maggie before Maggie found Mrs. Finch. "Please don't ask her to take you out of the orphans' act!" Lisa said. "Your father's going to want to see you perform."

"He could have seen me if he really wanted to."

Maggie was surprised to see tears appear in Lisa's eyes. "I didn't mean to act the way I did," Lisa said. "I—well, I guess I was jealous of you, Maggie."

Maggie blinked. "You were jealous of me? And all this time I was jealous of *you!*"

"Me? Why?"

"Well, you and Yolanda and Jo Beth and everybody else were having so much fun together."

"But you won the big part at the high school."

"I wasn't with my friends at the high school."

"What about Alex? I was so jealous when Alex hugged you."

"That was only one hug," Maggie blurted out. "I wish there had been more."

Maggie's voice had been so loud that some of the kids

who were passing by stopped and stared. Her cheeks burned as she leaned against the wall and took a long breath, trying to forget about Alex. It still hurt. "I really do want to work crew," Maggie said. "I thought about it all day. If my father had wanted to see me on stage, he had the chance. Come on with me while I tell Mrs. Finch."

But when they found Mrs. Finch backstage in the auditorium, she shook her head and rocked up and down on her toes. "There are two reasons why you should be in the orphans' scene, Maggie. For one, since the newspaper item gave the impression you'd have a role in the review, I think your father would be embarrassed if you weren't on stage. I even thought about the possibility of having you and Pete do one of the songs you performed in *Sound of Music*, but we don't have time for the band to get the music down pat."

"I don't want you to do a special favor for me or my father."

"It's not a special favor. It's a thrill for—well, for the school—to have a famous director see our production." She gave an extra bounce.

Maggie groaned. "I'd rather work crew."

"That's the second thing," Mrs. Finch said. "Today two eager volunteers asked to work crew, so I assigned them in your place."

"Who?" Maggie asked.

Mrs. Finch turned and searched among the students who were on their knees, painting banners. "Right over there," she said, pointing. "You know them. Jerico and Carter."

At the sound of their names both boys looked up from their work and smiled at Mrs. Finch. She smiled back.

But Maggie mumbled to Lisa, "What are they planning to do?"

Lisa stared. "They look wicked."

"I know."

Mrs. Finch looked at her watch and ran to center stage, clapping her hands and calling, "Everyone who is in the *Broadway Babies* scene, front and center."

Lisa and Maggie walked down to the front row of the auditorium and sat down to watch. "Alex moved away," Maggie said. "He didn't tell me he was going."

Lisa looked puzzled. "Why would he?"

"He said we'd always stay friends."

Lisa hunched her shoulders. "How could you? He was years older."

The band director finally got his students' attention, and music blasted through the auditorium.

Maggie didn't pay attention to the number. She thought how strange it was that Lisa, who was her best friend, hadn't understood, but Jerico, who was her enemy, had. And how, for a little while, Jerico had been her friend, and Lisa had not. And Alex—Maggie was glad Alex had been her friend, and she would never forget him. Ever. Maybe Jerico was right. Maybe she'd get Alex's address from Mr. Cassidy and write to him someday. And maybe she'd meet Alex again, and they'd both be glad. Maybe he'd be in films, even one of her father's films.

As she thought about her father, all the good feelings about Alex disappeared like wrappings on a package, leaving only a hard, angry lump. Maggie slid down in her seat, grumbling to herself. Now she wished her father wouldn't come to Houston.

Just as Grandma had predicted, a letter from her father was waiting for her when she got home after rehearsal. Maggie, holding it tightly, sat down at the kitchen table next to Annie Sue and Bonnie Joy, who were perched in their chairs on top of telephone books, contentedly munching cookies.

"Baby-sitting again?" she asked Grandma.

"They're such dear little girls," Grandma said. "I like having little girls in the house." She smiled at Maggie. "We'll be quiet while you read your letter."

With damp fingers Maggie opened the envelope, read the short letter, and shook her head, handing it to her grandmother. "Daddy says he's coming to Houston to watch me perform."

"I'm sure he had no idea that item would be in the newspaper before you got his letter."

"It shouldn't have been in the paper at all!" Maggie said. "Daddy never pays attention. I wrote about working crew for the musical review, and he still thinks I'm doing something with *Sound of Music*."

"Roger has a lot on his mind," Grandma said.

"But not me."

"Maggie, he loves you."

"Part of loving is paying attention. How can you love somebody and never listen to what they're saying?"

Grandma put a hand over Maggie's. "Part of loving is being patient, too. Please be patient with him. Whatever you do will make him proud. He'll be pleased that you've done a good job working crew."

"I'm not going to be working crew," Maggie told her. "Mrs. Finch stuck me in as one of the orphans in the 'Hard-knock Life' scene. I'm one of the orphans who comes in with a bucket of water and a mop."

Grandma beamed. "That was very nice of Mrs. Finch. Now Roger and Kiki *will* be able to see you perform."

Maggie flung her arms and head down on the table, forgetting it had been set for dinner. The plate wobbled as her forehead hit it, and a fork bounced to the floor. Annie Sue and Bonnie Joy whooped with laughter. "Kiki!" Maggie said as she sat up and grabbed for the knife and spoon. "I keep forgetting about Kiki. She'll be here, too!"

Grandma scanned the letter. "He doesn't say what flight they'll be on, just that they'll be staying at the Remington Hotel."

For a moment Maggie was hopeful. "Maybe they'll come on the wrong day!"

There was a light tap on the kitchen door, and Gloria came into the room.

Grandma jumped up to meet her. "Now, Maggie," she said over her shoulder, "he did remember the date of the play. It says so right in the letter." She turned to Gloria. "The girls were perfect little angels, as usual."

"Thank goodness," Gloria said. "You didn't have any trouble with Bonnie Joy?"

"Just one little accident," Grandma said, "but it wasn't her fault."

Gloria glanced at her youngest daughter and shrugged. "What play were you talkin' about when I came in?"

"Maggie's going to be in the school play."

"Wow!" Gloria said. "Another one? She'll be goin' off to Hollywood pretty soon."

Maggie shuddered. "I hope not!"

Grandma quickly said, "She's going to be one of the orphans in a skit from *Annie* in her junior high school musical review."

"I'd like to see that," Gloria said. "I went to one of those school things a couple of years ago, and there was whole families there. I could even bring the kids. They'd like the music."

"That would be lovely," Grandma said. "You could all come with us."

"If you don't mind the kids climbing all over everybody. Y'all know how they are."

Maggie giggled. She looked at Bonnie Joy, whose face was smeared with chocolate. She could just see her father with Bonnie Joy on his lap!

"We'll be there," Gloria said. "When you're on the stage, we'll all smile and wave at you, Maggie, and that will help keep you from gettin' nervous."

But as the Friday night performance grew closer, Maggie became more and more nervous.

She didn't have any trouble learning the dance steps for the orphans' song, and she already knew the words. Mrs. Finch had even told her how pleased she was with her performance. But Jerico and Carter were always nearby when she was on stage. They'd huddle together and look at her and chuckle as though they knew something she didn't know.

"They know what they're planning to do to me, and I don't!" Maggie told Lisa.

"I used to worry about what they'd do, but now I think they're all talk," Lisa said. "If they were really going to do something terrible to get even with you, they'd have done it by this time."

"Do you really think so?"

"Really. Stop worrying."

"What if they do something to spoil the performance?"

"They wouldn't dare."

"My father will be there."

"I told you, Maggie, stop worrying about them. What could they do?"

That was exactly what Maggie kept asking herself, and she couldn't find an answer. What could they do? What *would* they do?

But as opening night arrived, Maggie had too much to think about to include Jerico and Carter. Dennis came, with another bunch of chrysanthemums. Gloria arrived with Annie Sue and Bonnie Joy, who were so shining clean and tidy that their faces shone like pink china.

"I brought along toys and somethin' to eat to keep them quiet if they get fidgety," Gloria said. She studied Maggie. "You know, you're really gettin' close to skinny. But don't you think you'd better get fixed up pretty soon? You don't have much time left to change your dress and wash your face and comb your hair."

Maggie smoothed down her ragged dress. "It's my costume. I'm supposed to look messy and poor. I'm an orphan."

"I was an orphan, too," Gloria said, "and believe me, when we went out, we looked decent."

Grandma put an arm around Gloria's shoulders. "Keep in mind that Maggie's a character."

"She sure is," Gloria said.

Maggie couldn't help looking toward the door. "He isn't coming," she said.

"He'll come," Grandma said.

"Who?" Gloria asked.

"Maggie's father."

"That sounds kinda funny, an orphan's father."

"I want a cookie."

"Later. Mama's got lots of cookies in her handbag."

"Do you want me to call the hotel and see if Roger and his wife checked in, Momma?"

"No. They probably plan to meet us there."

"I don't think my father is coming."

"Calm down, Maggie."

"Cookie, Mama!"

"This is real exciting. The kids are gonna love the music."

Maggie opened the door. "Let's go. Mrs. Finch said to be there early."

Grandma took her hand. "I can't wait until you come on stage, honey. We'll be so proud of you."

The chatter kept up all the way to the school, and backstage everyone was trying to talk at once. Mrs. Finch popped up and down from group to group shushing and giving last-minute directions.

"Is your father here?" Lisa whispered.

Maggie just shook her head.

"I'm sorry," Lisa said.

"I wish our scene was on first," Maggie said, "so we could get it all over with."

The orchestra struck up the overture, and she could hear seats squeaking and feet shuffling in the auditorium as the audience settled down to listen.

The *Broadway Babies* number was first and got a rousing hand, even though one of the girls in the chorus tripped as she came offstage.

"I'd die if I did that," Maggie whispered to Lisa.

"You won't," Lisa said.

Mrs. Finch moved to stand beside Maggie. "I'd love to introduce your father after the performance, Maggie."

"He's not here."

"Are you sure? Why don't you look again?"

Mrs. Finch seemed so disappointed that Maggie obediently peeked through the small opening near the side of the curtain. The auditorium wasn't completely dark, so she easily found some of the people she knew. There was Mrs. Hardison, and behind her was Grandma and Gloria and—

"He's here!" she exclaimed so loudly that three of the people backstage scowled at her and made shushing sounds.

"Lovely," Mrs. Finch said and bounded to meet the second group who had finished their number.

"He's sitting next to Grandma with Bonnie Joy on his

lap, and a blond woman who's got to be Kiki is next to him," Maggie whispered to Lisa.

Lisa squeezed Maggie's hand. "I'm glad he came."

Mrs. Finch waved her arms in the air and hissed, "*Annie* group next! Ready?"

None of the girls needed to be reminded. They were already forming in line, Maggie at the tag end. Two of the crew members were handing out the props as the orphans trudged on stage. But just as Maggie reached out for her bucket and mop she heard a familiar voice.

"Well, well, here's Maggie!" Jerico said, and she saw the bucket swing upward. Suddenly, cold water drenched her. She sputtered and shook and pushed her dripping hair back from her eyes.

"You—you—!" she muttered. But she heard her cue, and she wasn't on stage. Time enough to take care of Jerico later. She couldn't let the others down. Maggie grabbed the empty bucket in one hand, the mop in the other, and dashed on stage, skidding and sliding out of the puddle of water.

The audience gasped, and Lisa's eyes grew even wider. But Maggie delivered her line, Lisa said hers, the orchestra began the first notes of the song, and all the girls—as though nothing had happened—began to belt out, "The Hard-knock Life."

Maggie threw herself into the song and didn't let herself worry about what her father would think. What difference did it make if he saw her at her worst? He should have come to *The Sound of Music*. And Jerico? Forget Jerico. He could take a long walk off a short pier!

It came as a surprise to Maggie that the audience was delighted. They seemed to be not quite sure if her dripping wetness was a comedy act or if she had been involved in the worst case of clumsiness on record, so they laughed and grinned and applauded like crazy when the number was over.

Mrs. Finch met Maggie with one of the large towels that was kept in the dressing room. "I'll find out later what happened," she said sternly, then gave a little hop. "At least the audience enjoyed it. Next group—on stage! Now!"

Maggie huddled inside the towel. There was no sign of Jerico and Carter.

Lisa took one end of the towel and tried to mop Maggie's forehead. "You were right to worry about them," she said. "I'm so sorry this happened to you!"

"Oh, Lisa," Maggie said, "I don't mind about me. I just didn't want it to spoil anything for you. You were wonderful."

"It didn't spoil anything," Lisa said. "It's not nice to say, but it really was funny!" She popped a hand over her mouth to suppress a giggle, then looked guilty. "Oh-oh. Your father," she said. "I wonder what he thinks."

"Shhhh!" someone whispered.

"It doesn't matter what he thinks," Maggie mumbled. But it really did. Her polished, always professional father probably thought she was stupid and clumsy and had let him down one more time. Maggie pulled the towel closer around her shoulders, ducking into it.

The group on stage changed places with the next group. The orchestra valiantly struck up their tune, hitting only a few sour notes in places where it didn't matter too much. The time went so fast that Maggie was surprised when Mrs. Finch, arms going like a windmill, waved them all on stage for a final curtain call.

Maggie, still wrapped in her towel, hung near the side of the stage, trying to duck behind the kids in front of her.

Mrs. Finch bounced to the center stage and held up her hands. All the lights in the auditorium came on. Immediately the applause stopped. She thanked the audience for their gracious attention, then said, "We have some distinguished guests with us tonight. I would like to introduce Mr. Roger Ledoux, who is a well-known Academy Award-winning Hollywood director."

Dramatically, she held out a hand toward Maggie's father, while the audience turned and stared and oohed to each other. Roger, who was in the process of gingerly handing Bonnie Joy to her mother, looked startled for a moment. Then he stood and nodded with dignity to Mrs. Finch and to the audience. Maggie gasped as she saw a large, wet stain where Bonnie Joy had been sitting on her father's lap.

"And his lovely wife, the actress Kiki Dillon," Mrs. Finch continued, blinking rapidly as she tried to pretend she didn't notice anything wrong.

Kiki stood, still holding Annie Sue. Kiki was tall and blond and even more beautiful than the photographs Maggie had seen. She was wearing a pale pink silk dress that was spotted with buttery smears and cookie crumbs. Just as Roger had done, Kiki bowed graciously, waving to the crowd.

"Thank you, thank you, all," Mrs. Finch warbled to the audience.

The cast ran off the stage to meet their parents. Maggie dashed to her father. "I'm sorry," she began. "I wanted to do everything just right, and I didn't—"

"Slow down!" Roger wrapped her in a hug. "I don't know what happened backstage, but whatever it was, you carried it off like a real pro. I'm proud of you!"

"But I was a mess!"

"Look at your father," Kiki said. "He doesn't look so great either." She brushed off the skirt of her dress. "In fact, right now I'm something of a slob myself."

Maggie couldn't help laughing.

"As far as slobs go, I'd say we're pretty special," Roger said.

"The slob family," Kiki said. She held out a hand to

Maggie, and Maggie took it, holding it snugly as she leaned into her father's hug.

"Roger and me, and Maggie makes three," Kiki sang.

Grandma was beaming at her, and Maggie smiled back. She knew this wasn't the happy ending to a fairy tale. There'd be lots of times when she and her father would be upset with each other, and she really didn't know Kiki at all. But at this moment, "and Maggie makes three," sounded just right.